"You're 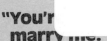 marry me."

Maggie flared up at his statement. "You've got it worked out, haven't you? It's the craziest thing I ever heard of."

"Why not, Maggie?" He sounded infuriatingly reasonable. "I can certainly look after you and Dixie far better than you can on what you're making."

She swung round furiously. "Dixie and I are doing just fine! We don't need you or anyone! I don't need a marriage. And I damn well don't need to shack up, either!"

"You're afraid, Maggie."

"No! There's nothing between us."

"Nothing?" he challenged. "Do you call a night in each other's arms nothing?"

VANESSA GRANT started writing her first romance at the age of twelve and hasn't forgotten the excitement of having a love story come to life on paper. Currently she teaches business at a community college, but she and her husband are refitting the forty-six-foot yacht they live on with their sons for a world cruise some time in the future. Vanessa believes in love. "After all," she confides, "the most exciting love story I know of is my own."

Books by Vanessa Grant

HARLEQUIN PRESENTS
 895—STORM
1088—JENNY'S TURN
1112—STRAY LADY

HARLEQUIN ROMANCE
2888—THE CHAUVINIST

VANESSA GRANT

takeover man

Harlequin Books

TORONTO • NEW YORK • LONDON
AMSTERDAM • PARIS • SYDNEY • HAMBURG
STOCKHOLM • ATHENS • TOKYO • MILAN

for Julie Ann

Harlequin Presents first edition June 1989
ISBN 0-373-11179-7

Original hardcover edition published in 1988
by Mills & Boon Limited

CHAPTER ONE

MAGGIE SIMPSON parked in the no-parking zone outside the post office, crossing her fingers and hoping no one would put a parking ticket on her government car.

She didn't have time to drive in circles looking for a place to park. She had to collect the mail and drive back to the wharfs before the fishing fleet started to come in.

She was the wharf manager, employed by the Canadian government's Fisheries and Oceans department. Her job was the dockside equivalent of landlord and maintenance person. She liked her work. It usually kept her busy, moving around the wharfs, looking after everything from sinking boats to rubbish left standing on the floats. She knew most of the fishermen and pleasure-boaters who came down to Rushbrooke floats, and most of them had a friendly word for her when they saw her. Even when the boat owners came to her with complaints, they usually had a smile for her.

Today her short, curly hair tumbled in the wind as she dashed inside the post office, the sun flashing red highlights that hinted at her temperament. She was shorter than average, but even in jeans and running shoes she was attractive enough to catch the eye of more than one man as she quickly emptied both her post box and Angus MacAvoy's.

She didn't look at the letters, but threw all the mail on to the car seat. She was on her way again before the traffic warden turned up, and she decided not to push her luck by making an illegal left turn on to Third Avenue—there was too much traffic, and she had already received one traffic ticket for trying to take the quick way back out of Prince Rupert's small downtown area.

A pedestrian activated the red light at the shopping mall crossing and Maggie took the opportunity to glance through her mail while she waited. A letter from her parents—postmarked three weeks ago. What mysterious route had it taken to travel five hundred miles in three weeks? Her bank statement. She tore open the envelope just as the light turned green, glanced at it quickly, half hoping to find an unexpected cash balance. She might as well hope to win the lottery!

She shoved the car into gear and promised herself that she would cover the bank overdraft on pay day before she went shopping for Dixie's school supplies. If she was lucky, there might be enough money left to make a payment on Dick's loan. She wished the damned loan would disappear as fast as the money did! She glanced down at the pile of mail, used her free hand to toss aside several brightly coloured flyers.

She changed lanes, signalled her left turn, and stalled the car just as the light turned red ahead of her. As if she were just learning to drive!

Under the flyers was a letter from Dick. Why did she feel such panic when she saw his handwriting? She got the car going again before she would let herself pick up the letter. The postmark said Seattle. So he was in the States, not back in Canada. She should have felt relieved, but the fact that he had written at all meant even Seattle was not far enough away.

She dropped it, unopened, as if not reading would make it go away. She picked up the letter addressed to Angus. His post-office box had contained a pile of advertisements, and one letter with handwriting she did not recognise. The address was written in thick black ink. From a man, she decided. A man who was sure of himself, confident and organised. No name on the return address. Just a street number. Would Angus recognise the handwriting?

At least it wasn't from his daughter. Last week his daughter and granddaughters had visited. The entire weekend had been a disaster. Angus didn't deserve such a selfish, pigheaded daughter as that! It had taken hours for Maggie to get a smile out of him after his visitors left.

She and Angus were neighbours and friends. Angus lived alone in the twenty-five foot sail-boat berthed on the last finger of Rushbrooke floats; Maggie and her daughter Dixie lived in front of him in a little house built on a barge. They had been living next door to each other almost four years, sharing the wharf and watching the world go by. Lately, since Angus had been having trouble walking, Maggie had taken to collecting his mail and picking up his groceries.

In some ways Angus behaved almost like family, helping Dixie with homework and coming for dinner most nights. Angus had his own family down south, a son and a daughter in Victoria, but up here Maggie and Dixie had adopted him. Dixie called her neighbour 'Grandpa Angus', and the old man smiled when he saw them.

By the time the light turned green, Maggie had almost managed to convince herself that the pile of mail did not include a letter from Dick waiting to be opened. Her car gained speed as she went down the twisted road to the waterfront.

A fresh north wind had turned the water white all the way from the government docks to the green tree-covered mountains on the other side of the harbour. It was August and the sun was shining, but the wind was cold. She could see two white sails moving on the water, leaning over in the wind. The clouds were moving fast across the green hills to the north. She could almost feel the soaring freedom of the clouds, and she knew that, outside the protected harbour, Chatham Sound would be filled with big, rolling seas.

When she pulled up to the main pier at Rushbrooke floats, she had to forget the sky and the fresh smell of the ocean on the wind, had to concentrate on the big, white yacht that had arrived in her short absence. It was berthed on the first finger, close to the ramp and the car park, and smack in the middle of the area reserved for commercial fishermen!

Her office was a small trailer on the main pier, but she hardly glanced at it now. Instead, she buttoned her denim jacket tightly and turned up the sheepskin-lined collar, then headed straight down the ramp to the boats. It was low tide, making the ramp steep and treacherous, but she was wearing running shoes with good grips so she was able to walk down quickly. She dodged around a man lugging an old outboard motor.

'Slow down, Maggie!' he teased as she passed.

'Never!' she retorted, and although she was smiling there was a flash in her eyes. She was getting ready to do battle with the captain of that white boat.

Perhaps she was a little psychic, because she had smelled trouble when she saw that boat. Had some instinct told her that the captain was an overweight tourist whose ego matched his waistline?

'You'll have to move,' she told him. She kept

repeating that, and he kept ignoring her. Her cheeks were starting to glow bright red and her eyes flashed her irritation, but he ignored that, too. 'This area is reserved for commercial fishermen,' she said with strained patience. 'If you would just move to the fifth finger, E float, then——'

'What do you mean, you don't have electricity?' he demanded belligerently. 'What kind of set-up is this?'

'Government wharfs.' She was an impatient girl, and this man was straining her sense of humour. She spoke slowly now, working on sounding reasonable. 'This is not a private marina. We don't have electricity on the floats, and what's more, this finger is reserved for commercial fishermen.'

She almost lost her temper when he shrugged and said, 'Never met a lady wharfinger before.' He was just the type to assume that a woman would not be able to handle the job.

Somehow she managed to smile at him, despite the sparkling anger in her eyes, managed to say with deceptive casualness, 'See that big boat at the cannery? Just over there—behind you. That's the *Haisla Warrior*. She's sixty-five feet long, filled with fish right now. Those other boats are waiting for her to unload, waiting their turn. Once they're unloaded, most of them will be steaming in through that breakwater to tie up here.'

He was looking faintly uncomfortable. Maggie suppressed an impish smile and added, '*Haisla Warrior* usually berths on this finger—right here—with her sister ship rafted up to her. Before dark you'll have two big boats outside you, men with boots tramping over your decks, fish-nets being let out on to the floats for mending.'

His stomach sagged over expensive white yachting

trousers. He glanced at the seiner, back at Maggie.
'Guess I should move before they get in here,
shouldn't I?'

'It would be a good idea,' she agreed, and that was
the end of that. She helped him tie up at his new
location and he unbent enough to smile and thank her
in the end.

Then she spent a few moments looking for Angus
before the fishing-boats started coming. She hadn't
seen him at all since she'd returned. The thought of
Angus's letter reminded her of the other mail, of
Dick's letter, waiting for her to open it. She wished
she could stuff it in the bin and pretend it had never
come. Or, failing that, she wished she had a date
tonight, something to distract her. Then she would
push the letter into a drawer and forget it until the
morning.

She didn't date very often. For a while last year she
had gone out with a local fisherman, then a doctor.
The fisherman had proposed marriage. The doctor
had wanted a serious affair, although he was divorced
and almost as wary of marriage as Maggie. She didn't
see either one of them any more. She hardly dated at
all now, except for a couple of friends among the
yachtsmen. Safe men, because they were usually
passing through and had no serious intentions.

The last thing in the world that Maggie wanted was
a serious affair or another marriage. The only good
thing that had come out of her marriage to Dick was
their daughter. Together, Maggie and Dixie were a
family, happy and secure.

In between the arrival of two small fishing-boats,
Dixie came back from swimming, flying down the
wooden wharfs in running shoes on bare feet, her
towel streaming behind her. Maggie barely had time

to ask, 'Where's your bathing suit?' before she turned back to the boats.

'Under,' said Dixie, grinning. Her body was starting to show curves Maggie hadn't expected to see for a couple of years yet. Her short, reddish-blonde hair was half-dry and wildly tangled. 'I was racing Betty out of the pool,' the young girl explained, her brown eyes filled with green glints of mischief.

Maggie felt a brief guilt that she hadn't managed to teach Dixie to be a little more organised, but there wasn't time for worrying today. She sent Dixie home to get the supper vegetables on the stove. Then, later, she found Angus standing on G float, his bushy grey hair falling over his forehead as he gestured to emphasise some point to the fisherman standing beside him.

'Letter for you!' she told the elderly man, digging the envelope out of her pack. His smile died as he held it in his hands. She almost asked him why, but someone called her name and she had to turn away. It was usually like that in the summer. Busy, having to run around while boats came and went in a constant stream. Next month it would be quieter, with the fishing season winding down and the tourists gone.

Two big American sail-boats came in. She guided them around the end of the main finger and rafted them together. Then she wandered up each finger, checking for potential problems, watching the sailors and fishermen visiting back and forth between boats. On the last finger she found Angus stepping slowly on to the dock from his cockpit. He'd been limping a lot lately. Arthritis, he claimed. She stopped beside him, her energy spent.

'Tired?' he asked quietly, his eyes smiling.

'Hmm.' She succumbed to a yawn. 'I'm going to

cook something delicious and fattening.' She thought
of her mother's overly generous proportions,
shrugged and said, 'Today I've done enough running
around to justify something good. Maybe hamburgers
to go with the vegetables Dixie's getting ready. What
do you think, Angus? Will you join us for dinner?'

He followed when she stepped on to her barge and
opened the door to the house. The outside of her
home needed paint badly, but the inside was warm
and friendly. She always enjoyed this moment,
coming inside, feeling the warmth of possession.

Security, she thought, looking around at the second-
hand furnishings, the pictures on the wall. Despite
the overdraft at the bank, they had security. She
owned the barge and house. The moorage was paid six
months ahead. Most important, she had a steady job.

It was later, when Dixie was in bed, that Maggie
and Angus sat out on her little patio. She brought a
beer for him, and a cider for herself. She loved the
sounds of the waterfront at night, the mysterious
shadows from occasional overhead lights.

'I got a letter from Dick today,' she said, her
strained voice destroying the silence. 'It's from
Seattle.'

He had been deep in his own thoughts, but after a
long pause he asked quietly, 'What does he want?' He
knew how upsetting Dick's letters were for her,
although there hadn't been one for almost two years
now.

She lifted the cider, sipped and concentrated on the
way the cool liquid tingled on her tongue. She would
give anything to have been able to tear the letter up,
unread. It would be like shutting a door on him, a
proof that Dick Simpson couldn't hurt Maggie any
more, yet it was an impossible fantasy. He was Dixie's

father, and for Dixie's sake the letters had to be opened. She took another big gulp of the cider, managing not to choke on it.

'Something's gone wrong. Maybe he's lost his job, or—I don't know what, but—just——' Her voice was tight, her eyes black in the shadows. 'He's decided all his problems would be solved if we were married again.'

Angus rubbed the cool rim of his beer can with his thumb. 'It's probably natural, Maggie. After all, you're still available and he knows that. If you married again——'

'No way, Angus!' She spoke too loudly in the darkness.

He didn't touch her, but his voice was a husky, gruff caress. 'This time, pick a man you can depend on.'

'I can depend on me,' she said flatly, her eyes avoiding his, watching the spotlight from a boat just entering the breakwater. A wave of moody music came to them from a nearby boat.

Angus said with studied casualness, 'My letter was from Mickey. My son.'

She hadn't recognised the handwriting, which meant the son didn't often write. She peered at him through the darkness. He looked small and weak and . . . old. 'What did he have to say?'

She thought he was changing the subject when he said, 'My daughter Heather didn't care much for all this.' He gestured helplessly at the shadowy boats and the water.

She said quickly, contritely, 'Dixie and I didn't help. It's the first time you've had a visit from her, and we really messed it up. I'm sorry——'

'No, Maggie. It wasn't your fault, and Dixie didn't

do anything that terrible. Unfortunately, my daughter has no sense of humour, and now she's managed to get Mickey worried about me.'

A diesel rumbled loudly as a big seiner slipped past to join the other fishing-boats. Maggie sat silently, letting the sounds of the waterfront flow over her, waiting for Angus to say what was on his mind.

'Everything was wrong for her, Maggie. The wharfs. The peeling paint on my boat. The noise. I saw her getting that light in her eyes—as if she were a missionary determined to spoil other people's fun.' His voice was frail and tired in the darkness.

A man's voice called out loudly. A quieter voice answered. Maggie cupped her hands around her glass.

Angus said musingly, 'I don't know how Sasha and I could have had a daughter like that . . . She thinks I should be put into an apartment somewhere—with walls and rules.' He picked up his beer, set it down again. 'As if I can't look after myself—and now Mickey's coming to visit.'

What did she know about Angus's son? Hard working. Smart. Successful. He had taken over Angus's quiet little electronics business and turned it into efficient modernity. But now Angus was pushing a worried hand through his grey hair, saying, 'If Heather went to work on Mickey, he might agree that I should leave the waterfront.'

'But——' She shook her head, not understanding this. Most Christmases he went to visit his children. The rest of the year he hardly mentioned them. 'Angus, they can't make you leave. Not if you don't want to.'

He picked up the beer can, then put it back down on the rail with a bang. 'Mickey always gets his way, Maggie. Even when he was small he would get that look on his face. He makes plans and—he makes his plan, and it happens. His way.'

She pushed her chair back, the angry, scraping noise echoing in her voice. He couldn't see the green fire flashing in her eyes, but he could hear it in her rising voice. 'Not this time, Angus! He won't get his way this time! If you want to stay, you're staying!'

'No, Maggie. You don't know Mickey.' He sounded so tired. His shadow settled lower in the chair. 'He'll look at all this—— Once he would have understood, but Mickey's changed. With his new lady—I met her at Christmas. He's living with her, and she's changed him. Heather says they're getting married soon. He's into management and high society and vertical integration.'

She blinked. 'Integration? That sounds like something a psychologist does, not an electronics engineer.'

She was thankful for the smile in Angus's voice as he said, 'Vertical integration. In other words, corporate takeovers. Mickey makes wind generators, so he's looking at buying out the manufacturers of the components he puts in the generators. Then, next, he buys the stores that sell the generators. By the time he's finished——'

She had heard enough. She shook her head vigorously. What little light there was caught the planes of her face. 'You may not be able to fight him, Angus, but I can! And I can be one tough lady!'

CHAPTER TWO

'HEY, mister! Don't step on my fish!'

Michael jerked to a halt, his immaculately polished shoes just inches away from an ugly, quivering fish. He found himself looking down at a barefoot young girl of eleven or twelve. Her golden urchin curls tumbled around a thin, enchanting face as she propped one end of her fishing-rod on her slim hip. She was barefoot on the bare wooden boards of the wharf, her feet as darkly tanned as her hands and face.

'Don't step on my fish!' she repeated. Her arm lifted the rod in a sharp jig as she stared up curiously at him.

'I won't,' he promised sincerely, eyeing the repulsive fish on the wharf. 'What is it?'

'Quillback.' She was very businesslike, her voice brisk, her tanned hands confident on the fishing-rod. 'Tastes good fried. My mom'll cook him. She's the wharfinger.'

'The what?' Unwillingly, he found himself fascinated by her.

'Whar—fin—ger,' she said patiently, reeling in her line and keeping her eyes on it to be sure it didn't tangle. 'She looks after the wharfs. You know—tells boats where to tie up, collects the money.'

'She might be able to help me, then.' He wasn't comfortable about this visit so, typically, he wanted to get on with it as quickly as possible. Yet he found himself strangely willing to linger and waste time talking to this self-confident young lady clad in faded

18

blue denim.

She caught the line with her hand, fastened the hook. She looked him over carefully, then said, 'She'll prob'ly help you. She helps everyone.'

He felt self-conscious under her intense examination. What was she seeing when she stared so hard? His dark blond hair brushed until the curls hardly showed? Grey eyes? Polished leather shoes? Light brown trousers and matching suit jacket?

Her brown eyes narrowed as they came to rest on his tie. Was he the only person who had ever visited the waterfront wearing a tie? He asked, 'Where would I find your mother?'

She frowned hard at the tie, said, 'If you're goin' on a fishin'-boat, you'll get dirty.' Her voice had cooled, as if she had decided that he did not belong here among the boats and fish-nets.

'Sail-boat,' he corrected. 'Not a fish-boat.' He gave himself a mental shake. It was crazy to be wondering if he measured up to this urchin's standard of dress. 'I'm looking for Angus MacAvoy's boat. Would you know which one it is?'

Her brown eyes widened, revealing flecks of green. She nodded, then busied herself picking up the revolting fish by slipping her fingers into the gills. Michael wished his fastidious nieces could see.

A man in a yellow mackinaw and tall rubber boots stepped off a nearby fishing-boat and called out, 'Hey, Dixie! How's the fishing?'

'Just a little quillback,' the girl shouted back. She held up the little monster.

The man grinned and shook his head. 'You can't eat that for dinner. How about this one? Make a nice meal for you and your mom?' He held out a small pink salmon and the girl ran over to take it quickly.

'Thanks, Mr Wilson!' she called back, then she was busy trying to get the two fish on to the fingers of one hand.

Michael offered, 'Can I carry something for you?' then regretted it when she offered him the quillback, warning, 'Y' got to watch his spines. They're poisonous.'

He had intended to offer to carry the rod, but he accepted the fish and managed to look reasonably enthusiastic. 'What do you want him for if he's poisonous?'

'*He's* not poison! Just the prickles. If they poke you, you get stung and it swells up and hurts.'

He held the spiny monster away from his suit. Would his dry cleaners be able to deal with fish slime? He asked her warily, 'How far are we going?'

She gestured vaguely with the rod, but from what he could see of the noise and confusion up ahead, Dixie seemed to be heading straight into a dockside fight. At the junction between the main float and the next finger, two big men were facing each other with anger and aggression written in every line of their bodies.

The woman standing between them was small and slender, yet generously endowed with womanly curves. She had her hand held up as if to make a barrier between the angry men. Her short curls glinted copper in the sunlight. Her face was mobile and expressive, filled with both laughter and tension. Michael had the feeling that he was seeing her frozen in the instant before an explosion.

The man doing the screaming was dressed in permanent-press trousers and a recently ironed shirt. His face was pale, an odd contrast to the woman's flaming hair and flushed face. His sleek, short hair was bristling as he shouted, 'Your God damned dog! If you don't get that bitch off the wharf, I'll have its hide!'

For a moment Michael thought the shouting was directed at the woman. Then he saw the other man shake back a generous head of hair and loop his fingers in the belt of tattered jeans. The shaggy man's voice was high-pitched as he glared at his accuser and screamed back, 'My dog doesn't mess on the docks!'

The woman braced herself, caught the offending dog by the collar and said, 'Take it easy, Solly.' The dog was motionless. Michael suspected that the woman would not be able to hold the animal if it wanted to move.

The sun escaping from a cloud overhead turned her short curly hair into a golden-red halo. She seemed to have cast herself in the dangerous role of peacemaker. Ahead of Michael, the girl named Dixie had stopped walking. Michael stopped too, and heard the woman say carefully, 'The mess is gone, Solly. You didn't step on it. You didn't fall in it.' The dog's owner opened his mouth, then closed it when the woman said sharply, 'Rex, don't you dare!'

The man named Solly glared at the dog. Michael saw the woman place one fist on her hip. His eyes followed the curve down from her buttocks, wishing he could see the legs under the denim. She managed to look both dangerous and enticingly feminine at the same time.

Her legs moved farther astride. She said, 'Solly, you know you can't kill the dog.' Michael could have sworn that she giggled, but she swallowed the sound quickly and said sternly, 'If you do, I'll make sure your boat never ties up here again!'

This had to be Dixie's mother, the lady who looked

after the wharfs. If so, she must have been a child bride. She couldn't be anywhere near thirty years old.

Solly was still screaming, accusing, 'Rex does this deliberately. I've put up with that damn dog for two years! I'm bloody well not going to——'

The woman's eyes flashed green as she interrupted sharply, 'If you don't like it, you can move your boat over to Fairview.' Solly's mouth hardened into a thin line, his jaw working under the skin, then he spun around abruptly and disappeared into his boat. The other man's grin faded as the woman turned to him and said swiftly. 'You'd better keep this dog out of the way, Rex!'

'Maggie, it wasn't——'

'Of course it was.' Her face lit with impish joy. 'Can you imagine it? Front page headlines in *The Daily News*. "Dockside murder as long-time resident goes on rampage against mongrel dog." ' The colour in her cheeks was still high, but her smile was gone as quickly as it had come. 'Rex, you know what a filthy temper Solly has. If you two want to start World War Three, you're not doing it here. You'd better follow that dog around with a shovel. And move your boat over outside *Karen A.*'

'Oh, hell, Maggie!'

She just shrugged and turned away, her smile breaking out again as she saw Dixie standing with the salmon in one hand and a fishing-rod in the other. 'Nice fish, honey. Who gave it to you?'

Dixie lifted the fish, examining it a little resentfully. 'How d' you know I didn't catch it myself?'

Michael found himself fascinated by two curly heads close together, two expressive faces. The woman's hair was darker than the girl's, her figure more mature, but no one who saw them together

could doubt their relationship. The mother pointed and
said, 'See the scars behind the gills? Those are marks
from the fisherman's net.' She straightened, seemed to
see the man with the unsightly fish hanging from his
fingers for the first time. Her eyes glinted in an
amusement that Michael found ridiculously irritating.

'I'm looking for Angus MacAvoy's boat.' He was
startled when her smile died and her eyes widened,
turning a deep green in the reflection of light from the
blue water around them. Why would the thought of
company for one of the boats disturb her? 'I take it
you know where his boat is?' he persisted, his voice
cool and businesslike.

'You're Mickey? Angus's son?' Her voice was high,
her eyes dark and deep. Perhaps she was not quite as
young as he had thought. When she frowned, the
colour left her cheeks and she might be thirty. Barely.

'Michael, not Mickey,' he corrected automatically.
He saw the brief laughter flash again in her eyes, and
he wished he had not made an issue over the use of his
childhood nickname.

'Yes, sir,' she said slowly, 'Mr MacAvoy.' He
couldn't actually be blushing at the ridicule in this
woman's voice, could he? Damn! He was thirty-seven
years old, and he couldn't remember when he had felt
so stiffly self-conscious before.

She turned away, said briskly, 'Dixie, I'll take the
rod. You take the fish—both of them—and head home
to clean them.' She glanced back at Michael with swift
appraisal, unable to suppress a smile as he eagerly
surrendered the quillback to Dixie.

The girl said, 'Bye!' and was off, a fish hanging
from each hand. Her mother said, 'Mr MacAvoy——'
but he corrected her quickly.

'Michael.'

He watched her take a slow breath, as if hardening herself for battle. Why hadn't he listened more carefully to his sister's chatter? Heather had said something about a woman. Had the name been Maggie? Just who was she? How did she fit into his father's life? An uneasy feeling was growing inside him. This weekend was not going to be as straightforward as he had thought when he got on the plane this morning.

Maggie was walking ahead, leading the way. He found himself watching her swaying hips.

Maggie walked quickly, as if she could escape him. He made her uncomfortable. He was well dressed, confident, handsome. None of that mattered. It was something else, a shock that surged through her body when his eyes met hers. She felt nervous and exposed.

She had a desperate urge to get away from his grey eyes and strengthen herself before she faced him again. She couldn't help feeling that he could see right through her, that he knew her self-confidence was only a façade. Could he know that she had vowed to fight him for Angus? She shook her hair back, felt his eyes touching her back. She tried to subdue her walk, but somehow knew that he was noticing even her discomfort.

She dropped back to walk beside him. Talk would be easier than silence, she decided. She asked brightly, 'Did you come in on the morning flight?'

'How else?' he asked, amused.

'Take a train . . . drive—I guess not, for a weekend trip.' Her voice quickened. 'It's about a thousand miles by road. You live in Victoria, don't you?' Darn! She was talking like an idiot, and he seemed to be enjoying her discomfort. 'What was your flight like?'

'Uneventful,' he said briefly. His mouth was hard,

not smiling, and he looked like a man who had little
patience for wasting his time. The more she chattered,
the quieter he seemed.

I'll shut up, she decided, but she was a talkative girl
and silence came hard. She wished that he were more
ordinary, like one of the men on the docks. She had an
uneasy feeling that Angus had been right. Michael
MacAvoy was not going to be easy to defeat.

She shifted the fishing-rod, concentrated on
watching the boats as they passed. She had every
reason to look away, study the vessels, ignore his
silent appraisal of her. She was the harbour
manager—the wharfinger. Most of the boating people
still retained the old name, even though the
government signs had changed 'wharfinger' to read
'harbour manager'.

They turned on to G finger. She would have led the
way, but Michael walked ahead, making straight for
Angus's sail-boat. When he stopped, staring at it,
Maggie knew he was seeing all the things that were
shabby.

Sasha's woodwork badly needed varnishing.
Maggie and Dixie had done some touching up in the
last couple of days, but the topsides still needed
painting. One section of lifeline was worn through
and hadn't been replaced. The docking lines had been
doubled up, but they would soon have to be replaced
with new lengths of rope.

He stepped closer to look down, seeing the wispy
green of underwater growth clinging to the
underwater hull. Angus hadn't had his boat out of the
water for anti-fouling in three years, and the neglect
showed. Maggie felt a sudden surge of anger flowing
through her veins. How dared Angus's son fly up
here, taking the early jet from the big city, bringing

his critical eyes and his cool voice? He was looking at
the sail-boat as if it were a factory he was planning to
take over and renovate. He didn't belong here!

She pushed her hands into her jeans' pockets and
tried to make her voice very casual, but the anger
showed. 'Why did you come up here? What do you
want?'

He was much more controlled, his face
expressionless as he turned to face her and ask, 'What
business is it of yours?' His voice was very soft, but
there was something in his eyes that was dark and
hard.

'Angus is my friend! I care about him!'
Unconsciously, her hands went to her hips and her
eyes flared, meeting his aggressively.

Then, unexpectedly, he smiled and said, 'Then
there's no problem, is there?'

'Isn't there?' She didn't let herself return his smile,
didn't let him see that she was irrationally tempted to
like him, despite his reasons for being here. She
mustn't let herself warm to him or she wouldn't be
able to help Angus. She turned away and knocked on
the boat's deck, called out, 'Angus! Your company's
here!'

She was relieved when the hatch slid back and
Angus's grey head came up, followed by the old man
himself. She was supposed to be the one protecting
Angus, but right now she almost felt like calling for
help herself and she didn't know why, any more than
she knew why Michael's eyes on her thoroughly
clothed body should bring heat to her cheeks.

Angus limped as he stepped out on to the wharf.
There was no point hoping that Michael wouldn't
notice. He seemed to notice everything. She
concentrated on getting her own reactions under
control. Now that she had met Michael, she knew she

would have a battle to defeat him in any bid for control over Angus.

The two men stood for a moment, staring silently at each other. They were unmistakably father and son. Both tall, although Michael was taller and straighter. Both fair, but Angus's hair hadn't been that shade of blond in years. Angus had deep lines on his face, but Michael's was only lightly lined, as if he controlled his life without unwanted stress.

They shook hands. Maggie knew that Angus would have welcomed an embrace from his son—something more than the casual, 'How are you doing, Dad?'

The older man's voice was strangely unconvincing as he said, 'Fine. I'm fine.' Maggie felt like shaking him. Didn't he realise that he needed to look strong and confident today? His voice was old and weak as he said, 'Come aboard, Mickey.'

She wanted to do something about it, to distract Michael from his critical survey of everything, including his father. She might have thought of something to say if the radio on her belt hadn't erupted with a blast of loud static and a voice calling, 'Rushbrooke harbour manager, this is the *Costa Brava.*'

Angus heard and said quickly, 'You'll come over later, Maggie?' and she could feel his tension.

'You can bet on it!' She made her voice confident, telling him without words that opposing Michael would be a cinch. 'Don't forget you're having lunch at my place—both of you. I'll call you when it's ready, Angus.'

Michael interrupted, saying politely, 'Thank you, but we'll have lunch on our own.' He turned away as if there could be no argument.

Maggie could see the worry in Angus's eyes, and she knew that she couldn't let him win, no matter how nervous he made her feel. Before he could disappear into the sail-boat, she said quickly, 'Don't worry about it, Mr MacAvoy. Your father is like a member of my family. Of course you'll both have lunch with us.'

She swung away before he could answer her. If he did say anything, she blocked it out by taking the radio from her belt and speaking clearly into it, 'Costa Brava, Rushbrooke. Go channel sixty-eight.' She could already see the bulk of the large, white yacht *Costa Brava* approaching Rushbrooke floats.

She glanced back as she started to turn the corner on to the main float. She was disconcerted to find Michael watching her. She had the uneasy thought that she could read his mind, that he was analysing just what effect she was going to have on his plans. For a long moment they stared at each other along the length of the float.

'Not close enough to see the whites of his eyes,' she murmured, then had the disquieting feeling that— impossibly—he could hear. She simply had to stop feeling so unnerved by him! She turned away decisively and concentrated on finding space for the boat that was coming in.

By the time she was ready to start cooking lunch, Maggie had regained her usual self-confidence. She decided to cook the salmon, ignoring the uncomfortable conviction that Michael might realise it wasn't strictly legal for fishermen to be giving away net-caught fish. She made herself ignore a fleeting desire to arm herself with expensive clothing and a subtle, confidence-building layer of make-up. She had no time in the middle of a busy day for dressing and making-up!

When lunch was almost ready, she sent Dixie over to Angus's boat *Sasha*, to call the two men. She wondered if Michael might not persuade Angus not to come to lunch after all, and she wasn't sure what she would have done if they had not come.

Angus was uncharacteristically silent as he came through the door. His hand was linked with Dixie's, but Dixie and Angus both seemed to be inhibited by Michael's cool, grey eyes. Couldn't the man see that his presence was disturbing his father? Disturbing Maggie, too. He was looking at everything from the instant he came through the door, seeing too much. His eyes crossed hers, but there was no smile in them.

He must be like this in his boardrooms, winning his corporate battles. His face was very still, masking his thoughts. Everything was under control. Even his well-brushed hair showed only a hint that it might want to spring free and curly. She knew he was making judgements about her, drawing evidence from his intent examination of everything in this tiny home of hers.

Darn the man! She loved her house, and normally she only opened her door to people she liked. This was the first time she had had to watch anyone criticising her home with cold, piercing eyes. He was seeing the cracked window, the ceiling that needed painting after the leak that had developed last summer. She had managed to fix the leak with the help of a fisherman friend, but the painting would have to wait for a winter day when she wasn't so busy.

Without saying a word, he was making her see all the shabby details of her home, and she had an angry desire to shout at him, to tell him with wild, furious words that this was a home, a place she and Dixie and Angus loved and shared.

She had bought the comfortable old chesterfield set from a wonderful couple who were retiring to a condominium in Florida. She had found the old oak sideboard in a garage sale, and had worked on it for weeks to restore it to polished beauty. The paintings on her wall were a gift from a penniless artist friend who had slept on her living-room sofa for two months while he looked for a job. The sea-shell collection on the shelves near the window had been growing for years, added to by friends who knew she loved collecting. She hated watching him examining it all.

'This is nice,' he said after a long moment. He was standing in front of the sea-shell collection and he sounded surprised.

'We like it,' she said stiffly, trying to shut him out with her voice.

'Abalone?' he asked, picking up a shell. He looked at her, his eyes startlingly warm and curious.

'Yes.' She moved closer, feeling her rigid shoulders relaxing slightly. The shell collection was a safe topic of conversation.

He said wonderingly, 'I didn't think they came that big in the north Pacific.' She watched his long fingers caressing the blue and rose patterns of mother-of-pearl on the abalone.

'They don't,' she agreed, softened by his evident love of the beautiful shell. Watching his hands, she found herself wondering how it would feel if he were to caress her skin with that slow, gentle motion. Her thoughts made her voice uncomfortably breathless. 'The one you're holding is from California. A friend gave it to me.'

'A friend?' She flushed at the speculative tone in his voice. He thought the friend would be a man, her lover. She knew she was right when he asked abruptly, 'Where's Dixie's father?'

Dick was Dixie's father. She hoped he was still in

Seattle. Ever since she had got the letter from him, she had tried to ignore a nagging worry that he was on his way back to Prince Rupert. Now her thoughts were caught in her eyes, and Michael seemed to be reading them, making judgements. She sucked in a ragged breath and made her voice hard.

'Is that any of your business?' If anyone else had asked, she would have said casually, 'We're divorced.' She might have added, 'It was a long time ago.' But when Michael MacAvoy asked the question, she felt ridiculously panic-stricken. How was she going to help Angus when he had such an unnerving effect on her?

She moved away from him, becoming aware of Angus and Dixie talking quietly at the table. Maggie said brightly, 'I'll get lunch on the table shall I?'

There was an uncomfortable silence as Michael came to the table, until Dixie turned to Angus and said, 'Solly and Rex are fighting again.'

The old man sat straighter, his eyes focusing and his lips curving in anticipation as he asked, 'What did Rex do to aggravate Solly this time?'

Dixie said, 'The dog again.'

Maggie explained to Michael, 'The argument you saw today isn't new. Solly and Rex are the original odd couple.' Angus was listening, smiling, so she went on, 'Rex is a leftover from the hippie generation, and Solly is as straight as they come. They can't look at each other without abrasion, but they can't seem to stay away from each other either.'

Maggie relaxed a little as lunch went on, thinking that the conversation must be showing Michael how his father loved this life. It was like a cold shock to her when Angus mentioned Christmas, and his son murmured, 'Cold winters,' glancing at her for confirmation. That was when she realised that she couldn't afford to relax without Michael taking advantage. He would use anything for his own purposes, and she was certain that Angus was right in his estimation. Michael's purpose was to take his father away from this place.

'The winters aren't that cold,' she denied hurriedly. 'It freezes, but we don't get much snow here. Some years we get none.'

Angus was toying with his food. Michael said very casually, 'No harm thinking about a move, Dad. You remember how mild Victoria's winters are.' Then he firmly changed the subject before Maggie could say a word.

He spent the rest of the lunch hour talking with Dixie, collecting a great deal of seemingly unimportant information about their life. Dixie regretfully denied being twelve years old and admitted to being eleven—almost. Then she explained that their electricity came from batteries charged by solar cells. Grandpa Angus had installed the solar system for them two years ago, before his arthritis started to bother him.

His eyes met hers as Dixie explained about their electricity. She wished she could stop Dixie's chatter, because Michael was going to use whatever he learned against them. Somehow he knew that she intended to fight him over Angus.

By old custom, Angus and Dixie moved to wash the dishes after lunch. Maggie was left alone with Michael.

'I make you nervous, don't I?' he asked in a low voice when they were alone.

She said abruptly, 'I don't trust you,' and was shocked at her own words. He smiled as if her discomfort amused him, and she could feel the heat rising in her own face.

She turned away, moving quickly into the kitchen area. 'I'll take over the dishes, Dixie. You'd better get ready for your swimming class.'

Michael crossed over to her bookcase. She knew it was crazy, but she wanted to shout a protest when he picked up one of her favourite books to read. As she worked on the dishes with Angus, Maggie couldn't help feeling that he was listening to every word they spoke. Her eyes kept returning to him, wondering what he was planning as he pretended to read.

She was relieved when the door closed behind her guests and she could go back to work herself, yet all afternoon she kept worrying about what Michael might be saying to Angus.

She was distracted from her worry when a familiar boat came in from an Alaskan trip. She helped berth the large steel sail-boat, then shared a big hug with the captain's wife, her old friend Jan.

'How's your love-life?' asked Jan confidentially when they were alone for a moment.

'So-so,' said Maggie. She wished she didn't have a sudden fanciful vision of herself in Michael MacAvoy's arms. What was it about the man? His grey eyes were cold, for heaven's sake! Why did she fantasise about him touching the places his eyes had been on as he watched her trying to deal with Solly and Rex?

'No dates?' asked Jan, her voice just a little critical. 'Maggie, you should find someone. You've hardly dated since that fisherman last year. He was nice and——'

'He wanted to get married,' said Maggie defensively. She had enjoyed his company until then, but another marriage was the last thing she wanted. 'I've been invited dancing tonight,' she said quickly.

She had almost forgotten with the events of the day, but yesterday her friend Darryl had sailed into port for the first time in months.

'Oh?' Jan made it a question.

Maggie said, 'Darryl. Remember, you met him last spring?'

'The American who makes his living delivering boats?' Jan grinned, said speculatively, 'Tall, dark, handsome and dangerous-looking?'

Maggie laughed. 'I'm in no danger from Darryl. He's in town, and he asked me out, but I don't think I should go. Angus usually babysits for me, but he's busy tonight. His son's visiting.' An image of Michael came strongly into her mind, and she hardly heard what Jan said.

'What?' she asked, confused by her own thoughts.

'I'll babysit for you—it'll give me a lovely chance to sit back and read a good book without any interruptions. What are you wearing? I've got just the thing!'

'You would,' said Maggie, laughing. 'I suppose you've been hitting all the garage sales up there in Alaska?'

'Of course! Come and see!' Jan lifted a mattress and a hatch cover, then pulled out boxes and bags until she unearthed a dazzlingly frothy creation that was made for Maggie. She stared at it critically, said, 'It needs ironing, but——'

'It's gorgeous,' breathed Maggie.

'Three dollars,' said Jan smugly. 'It was hanging on a hanger among a bunch of old-fashioned dresses.'

'I'll have to fight Darryl off.' In Jan's mirror the dress seemed to intensify the green of Maggie's eyes and bring her hair alive with gold highlights. 'I look very expensive—except for the running shoes.'

Jan, of course, had a pair of flimsy, golden slippers that matched the belt of the dress. Maggie thought Jan could probably dress a movie star and no one would know that the whole ensemble had cost five dollars instead of five hundred. When Maggie left Jan's boat, she carried an armful of frothy creation back to her barge, grinning when she encountered a fisherman friend.

'Cinderella,' he speculated, appreciating the contrast between the dress and her blue-denim-and-running-shoes ensemble.

'Only until midnight,' she shot back, laughing, but she was glad the evening's dancing was going to become a reality. The contact with Angus's son had shaken her self-confidence, and there was no one like Darryl for making her feel pretty and feminine.

When Dixie returned from swimming, Maggie told her that Jan and her family had arrived. The girl went tearing over to spend what was left of the afternoon with Andrea, Jan's daughter.

Maggie hung up the dress and decided to go back to work. Saturday wasn't an official working day for her, but she found it useful for catching up the details that often got neglected in a busy week. She collected moorage from several transient vessels, left notes on others requesting payment. In between collections, she slipped into her house and pressed the dress.

That evening, before getting ready for her date, she went over to Angus's boat. She had been a little worried all afternoon. Several times she had thought of stopping in to check on Angus, but she was not quite sure what pretext she could use. Normally, she wouldn't need an excuse for visiting, but with Michael there it was different.

The sail-boat *Sasha* moved gently, responding to

the movements of the men inside. Overhead, the sun
shone on the water, throwing a brilliant blue glare
into Maggie's eyes. She could hear them talking from
outside—or rather, she could hear Michael's voice.
His words confirmed her worst fears.

' . . . for a while and see how you feel about it.' His
voice sounded so cool, so rational, and when she heard
Angus murmur an indistinct answer she knew that
Michael was succeeding in taking over his father's life
without much of a fight.

Michael's voice again, brisk and efficient. 'I'll look
after it. We can fly back tomorrow, get you settled
into the house. I'll look after the rest. Sam's looking
forward to your coming.' Maggie thought there was
something odd in Michael's voice as he made the last
statement. She felt a sudden certainty that Michael's
live-in lady was not at all enthused about having
Angus come to live with them.

A speed-boat roared past, drowning out Michael's
words. She stepped on to the deck. Michael's voice
stopped.

'Permission to board?' she called out, not waiting
for an answer. Angus always welcomed her.

Michael didn't. She came through the hatch and
down the steps, coming to a stop face-to-face with
Michael. His father was seated at the small table, but
Michael was standing, ready for action and frowning
darkly. He was furious at her bursting in. He barely
managed to conceal his cold anger as he said tightly to
his father, 'I'll go and see about the tickets.'

She should have come sooner. She had thought
there was more time, but Michael had settled
everything in just a couple of short hours. Maggie
shifted, blocking his exit and hiding her nervousness
as he moved towards her. He seemed uncomfortably

large in the small boat. Would he physically push her aside?

Her voice was high-pitched, her words quick. 'Angus, is this what you want to do? Do you want to leave?' She tossed her curls back, suddenly glad to see the anger in Michael's eyes. That cold control frightened her, but anger she thought she could deal with. She smiled as his voice came with cold fury.

'Listen, Mrs—Maggie. This is our affair. A family matter. I'd appreciate it if you'd give us some privacy.' He stepped closer, towering over her, but Maggie stood her ground.

'Angus?' she demanded, her eyes never leaving Michael's face. For a long moment she thought Angus wouldn't speak.

Then he said slowly, 'I'm happy here,' and Maggie smiled at Michael, confident that she had won this battle.

'Dad——' he began, but Maggie pushed between them, her fists on her feminine hips, her eyes flashing green fire at him. 'He wants to stay! He's happy here and he wants to stay.'

Michael said coldly, 'I've had about enough of you, Maggie whatever-your-name-is!'

He stepped closer to her, towering over her, deliberately threatening. She wavered, then stiffened. It took every bit of control she had, but she smiled and said softly, 'If you've had enough of me, Michael MacAvoy, then leave. This is my place.'

She had thought him controlled, but he was shouting, 'If anyone leaves, it should be you! *This* is my father's boat!' He got his voice almost under control, finished coldly, 'And it's obvious that he can't look after it.'

Michael frowned, furious with himself at his

outburst.

What the hell was getting into him? Hadn't he learned more than this in his years of playing strategy games in business? He smoothed his face, subdued the anger and said very quietly, very rationally, 'Dad, it's time you moved closer to your family. Move into your old house. There's lots of room. We'll put your boat in Oak Bay Marina, hire someone to fix it up, do the bottom. It's ages since it's been done.'

Maggie interrupted hotly, 'He's doing it next week! Next week the high tides are coming, and Angus is putting the boat on the grid.'

Michael kept his sanity by keeping all his attention on his father. Angus said slowly, 'That's right. Next Saturday. I'm taking it out on the grid.' Michael was convinced that his father was lying.

'You can't——'

Maggie interrupted, getting her flushed face between Michael and his father again. He had an insane urge to take her face in his hands and kiss those full lips into silence. She said hotly, 'Want to bet? Come back in two weeks. You'll see it then, all painted and pretty. You don't know much about boats, do you, Mickey?' She saw his irritation at the use of his nickname, grinned and said, 'You're fooled by the lack of a bit of paint. A boat needs tending every year. The elements are hard on paint, but a day on the tidal grid with scrub brushes and then some bottom paint, and she's as good as new.'

He took a deep breath, said with forced calm, 'Are you staying here all evening?' He wished he knew what her middle name was. Surely everyone had a middle name they hated? If he knew hers, he would use it now.

She smiled grimly. 'Are you going to force Angus to

go with you against his will?'

'I didn't come here to force him to do anything!' He didn't realise what violence he'd spoken with until she stepped back, away from him. She covered her nervousness quickly, smiling saucily at him, then turning to go over to Angus and bend down to kiss his cheek.

'See, love,' she said softly to the old man. 'It's all right. He's not going to make you leave your home.' Then she said quickly, breathlessly, 'I'd better leave while I'm ahead, hadn't I?'

And she was gone.

CHAPTER THREE

MICHAEL was far too restless to go to bed early. When his father retired, he went outside walking.

A curious quiet descended over the waterfront as dark fell. Once or twice Michael saw shadowy figures sitting outside on deck. Through the lighted window of one large yacht he saw a family watching television in a luxurious salon. Daytime had made a community of the fishing-boats and yachts, but darkness seemed to throw an impenetrable blanket over them.

Despite an occasional glimpse of other people inside their boats, Michael felt a sense of isolation, as if he were walking through this waterfront world as an observer.

The silhouette of a massive, long-necked bird was poised motionless on one of the breakwater logs, in black contrast against a slate-grey, moonlit sky. The bird watched Michael as he stopped beside the barge that held Maggie's house. Light shone through the curtains.

Was it Maggie's shadow he saw inside? Or Dixie's? It wasn't much of a house they lived in. Even in this light, he could see that it needed painting. It was only a wooden barge, and for all he knew the hull might be full of toredo worms. Certainly, it must be inconvenient living here, a long walk from shore whenever she bought groceries.

She had electricity to a limited extent, but only because his father had been good enough to set up a solar system for her. Had she paid for the solar plates?

Or had Dad paid? He tried to remember, because the plates must have been ordered from his firm, yet Michael couldn't remember the transaction at all.

What kind of woman was she, living with her daughter at the edge of the water as if she were an equal to the rough men who made their living from the sea? A tough lady, despite the enticing curve of her buttocks and the thrust of full breasts.

Not like Samantha. Sam had a lean, cool feminine grace. Michael would never describe Maggie as cool. She had probably driven Dixie's father away with her aggressive fire. An unwilling image of Maggie overtook him, her lips flushed with passion, her clothing tumbled by a man's impatient hands.

She was a witch, a fireball who hardly came to his chin. He had only met her today, but his hands wanted to touch her as if she were someone he had been wanting a long time. He swung away from the beckoning light in her window, pushing down the erotic fantasies that were fleeting through his mind as he stood here in the darkness outside her home.

He knew little about her, but it was quite possible that she was using his father. Dad had a comfortable income from investments, as well as regular dividends from Pacific Energy Systems. Was he supporting Maggie and Dixie? The woman had a government job, probably received a reasonable pay cheque. If she was getting extra money from somewhere, it didn't show in her dress or her home, and yet . . .

Unwillingly, he admitted that the interior of her unusual home was warm and interesting. None of the furnishings were new, but they were comfortable. Then he remembered the paintings on her wall. He had recognised them as Kealy's, and Kealy was becoming very popular. They wouldn't have been cheap. Had Dad bought the paintings for her?

Damn! He didn't want to know, didn't want to think about it. What had Heather talked him into, coming up here to manipulate his father's life? Why not leave him here in peace? But he knew the answer.

The boat was only one symptom of the ageing process, but a graphic one. The last time Michael had seen the boat, it had been shining and immaculate. Now it was shabby, and Dad hardly seemed to realise it. Soon he would need a cane for walking. Arthritis? Surely he should see a doctor? It was time for his children to take a hand in his life again, even if it meant getting into a battle with Maggie Simpson.

Michael turned away from the darkened barge and went back to *Sasha*, knowing he wouldn't solve any problems tonight. Maggie had made that impossible. Tomorrow he would go back home, then he'd work out a plan of action. Perhaps Pacific Energy Systems could provide the answer. Could he somehow use the business to lure Dad back to Victoria? If Angus thought his help was needed . . .

Yes, that was the line to take.

He dug through his father's ice-box until he found a can of beer. Then he settled himself in the cockpit, leaning back in the shadows.

Hypnotic silence filled with water sounds. Michael drifted, a warm content slowly surrounding him. He felt a strange unwillingness to face the thought of tomorrow, of stepping on to the jet and going home to Victoria.

Sam, he thought deliberately, but somehow the image of Sam's cool, blonde beauty evaded him. Perhaps it was the quality of the silence, the hypnotic spell cast by the lights streaking across the still water of the harbour, but he couldn't bring Samantha's image to life here. He settled comfortably in the corner of the cockpit, watching and listening, oddly content in his inactivity.

Eventually he heard the sound of footsteps, slow and leisurely. A low laugh, then a deep voice carrying indistinctly through the darkness. Michael's awareness focused sharply on a tall man moving slowly along the float. Beside him was a woman wearing some flimsy, frothy creation. Their hands were linked, swinging together slowly.

The man's voice again, almost loud enough to make out words.

Hers, clear and laughing. 'I dare you!'

They turned to face each other, then merged together, dancing to music Michael could not hear, floating over the planks, the man's hand at the back of her waist, holding her close.

Her arms slipped loosely around his neck. She was humming softly as they danced into the beam of an overhead light. Her hair glistened copper and gold in the light, telling Michael what he'd already known.

Maggie. The tough, vibrant wharf lady he'd seen earlier was dressed in froth and lace, floating across the planks in a bewitching dance with her escort. Was this Dixie's father? He was tall and dark, dressed in what looked like a quality suit, even in this half-light. The light beam played on a darkly tanned face. A fisherman or a sailor, Michael decided then. Whoever he was, he was totally intent on the woman in his arms.

Michael tensed, resisting a primitive urge to leap out of the cockpit and pull her away, into his own grasp. They had no idea they were being watched.

She was dressed for love. And in a mood for love, he decided, watching her twist away from the arms that held her, swirling in a solitary dance until strong arms pulled her back. Then the man's head bent low, shadows blending together. Michael felt his fingers tightening on the beer can and forced himself to relax.

Why didn't they go inside, out of his sight? Or why couldn't he tear himself away and go below, leave them to their loving?

The man's head lifted. His voice murmured. She laughed softly, shaking her head.

'Maggie——'

She said something, then raised herself on tiptoes to brush her lips on his. Then she slipped away and left her escort standing alone, looking after her.

Michael had the warped satisfaction of knowing he wasn't the only man who would be frustrated tonight. The tall man laughed ruefully, then disappeared into a large power-boat on the other side of the float.

Was he a neighbour, a regular resident of these docks? No. Earlier, Michael had noticed a customs permit in the window of that yacht. An American boat in transit. So Maggie dated men who were passing through, then left them frustrated on the wrong side of her door.

And what kind of a mother was she? She'd evidently left her young daughter to fend for herself while she stayed out long after midnight. Why did she have to call herself Maggie? Her name must be Margaret. Perhaps if she used it, she'd become more demure, more biddable, less of a wildcat.

What was it about this woman that seemed to arouse such uncontrollable emotions in him—feelings and urges he had no desire to feel? He was a rational man who prided himself in planning, analysing. He was a scientist, yet practical enough to succeed in business. He wanted his life and his mind to operate as his business did, with predictable challenges that could be mastered with energy and intelligence.

Light streamed across the finger as the door of her house opened. Maggie again, still in high heels and lace. Was she going to the American's boat? He hoped not. He didn't want to sit here, watching the darkened power-boat across the float, imagining her and the dark man locked in passionate embrace.

No, there was someone else, another woman at her side. The door closed. They talked, standing side by side on the floats. Michael heard the odd word. The woman's name was Jan.

' . . . thanks . . . should do it more often . . . driving inland tomorrow . . . the dress.'

Jan shook her head and laughed, said, 'Keep it! It looks good.' They sounded like old, warm friends.

So he had been wrong in his suspicion earlier. Maggie hadn't left Dixie alone, after all. The two women walked together down the planks, Maggie's high heels sounding clearly on the wood until she stopped to watch Jan walk away. Then she came back slowly, pausing as she drew abreast of the cockpit where Michael sat in the shadows. A light wind moulded her skirt against her legs as she stared into the darkness of Angus's boat. Her quiet voice carried clearly.

'Is this your usual style? Peeping Tom?'

He came to his feet silently, stepped over the side of the boat and on to the wharf. He felt as if his motions were pre-ordained, knowing he must touch her, feel her lips under his, her body soft yet wild in his arms. In high heels, the top of her head came just above his mouth. He restrained a strong urge to simply pull her close and bury his face in her glistening hair. He pushed his hands into his pockets, kept his voice cool.

'You didn't put on much of a show, Maggie. Is that all he ever gets? Just a kiss and a quick feel, then goodbye?'

She grinned, not letting his words hurt, tossing her head and sending the curls flying. 'You'll never know, will you, Mr MacAvoy?' Her rapid, shallow breathing thrust soft breasts against the bodice of that witch's dress. His eyes locked on the moonlit, creamy smoothness above the fabric.

Words tumbled past his lips without thought. 'What about Dixie's father? He's a sailor, I suppose?' He leaned closer, let her feel his breath on her cheek as he taunted, 'Off sailing, is he, Maggie? Do you play around while he's gone? Or do you just tease the men? That's better, isn't it? That way you're faithful—technically.'

She gasped. He saw a brief spasm of pain cross her face, then disappear so quickly that he wondered if he'd imagined it.

'You really are a peeping Tom, aren't you, Mickey boy? What's the matter? Doesn't your live-in lady give you what you need? That's too bad! But don't line up here if your sex life is lacking! I'm not so desperate that I'd invite in the likes of you!'

His arms flashed out and caught her shoulder. She jerked away, only to find herself suddenly imprisoned as both his strong arms encircled her. He pulled her closer, his nostrils breathing in an elusive, spicy scent of fire and erotic promise.

She twisted, soft curves pushing against him. He tightened, trapping her hands at her sides, feeling a primitive surge of triumph as he realised she was helpless in his arms. Entrapped she stared up at him. In the half-light, he couldn't make out the expression in her eyes, but he felt her heat.

'Let me go!' she muttered, her voice too husky for true anger.

He laughed softly, possessed by the devil she aroused in him. 'No way, Maggie. Not until I've had my turn!'

Her parted lips tasted faintly of cherries. His fingers spread on her back, soaking up the heat of her woman's flesh through the thin dress. He deepened the kiss, his tongue invading. She was warm, wonderfully right against his chest. He bent to take her mouth more deeply, his thigh moving against her leg, rustling the fabric of her skirt. He felt the faint abrasiveness of the gauzy dress, a sensual contrast to the softness he knew must be beneath it.

He staggered from the combined onslaught of his thoughts and the feel of her body. His outspread hands slipped down, curving over her buttocks, drawing her closer, her arms still trapped. The world was gone. There was a roaring in his ears. The feel and scent of an irresistible woman, soft and desirable and——

Pain jerked him harshly back from spinning, all-consuming passion. His arms tightened in spasm, rock-hard. The agony mingled with the pleasure of her warm body crushed against his chest. Then pain overwhelmed everything as her teeth dug sharply into his lip in an agonisingly painful attack.

'God damn it! You bit me!'

He rubbed his lip with cautious fingers, the red haze of pain receding, his eyes gradually narrowing on the woman in front of him. She was standing with the dress swirling around shapely legs planted astride, hands on her hips. Her lips were parted, her breath coming fast. A light from overhead showed her cheeks flushed with colour.

'I told you to let me go!' She sounded surly, like a defensive child.

He rubbed his lip cautiously, said resentfully, 'You could have said it a bit louder. You could have given me some warning that you're a man-eating tiger.'

Would her teeth marks show on his lip? She probably had very feminine teeth. Like a brand on him, for God's sake! Sam would notice, and she would be sure to ask about it.

What happened to your lip, Michael?
Maggie bit me.

He couldn't think of one innocent explanation for a bruised, split lip. Damn her! She could have got him somewhere it wouldn't show! Inexplicably, he laughed. Maybe the laughter was insanity, because a man had to be loony if he wanted a woman after she rejected him as painfully as Maggie Simpson had rejected Michael MacAvoy.

Her voice rose in resentful accusation. 'I should warn *you?* You're the one who should carry a warning! You should have it written on your chest—"Warning! This man takes what he wants without asking!" ' She shook her hair back, as if preparing to attack. 'Where I come from, a woman doesn't have to be forced into a man's arms just because he feels like proving he's a virile animal! You sure proved it, Mickey boy! You're a real man! You can grab a woman and haul her into your arms and force your lips on to hers.' Her laugh ended on a soft gasp as he stepped closer. 'One thing, Mickey. I bet the women you're used to don't bite!'

Before his outstretched hand could grasp her again, she was gone in a swirl of gauze. His sanity returned—slowly. He stared at his hands, flexing the fingers, remembering how those hands had grabbed her, taking, wanting.

He wanted to burst through her door, force her to accept an apology, in the hope that it could wipe out the memory of himself gone wild, caressing her body as if it were his possession. But he suspected that she did not want him to forget. She'd left her mark on him, for remembrance.

Had he really expected her to come into his arms with the warm willingness she'd given to her date? Had he thought—— No! Hell! He hadn't done any thinking, just wanting and grasping, like an undisciplined child.

It was time—way past time for him to go to bed. But of course, he couldn't sleep at all, although he did finally manage to achieve calm by forcing himself to think about Rory Pederson. Rory had listened to Michael's takeover proposal earlier in the week—listened, and been impressed. They'd talked until Rory's staff had gone for the night, then Rory had taken Michael home and they'd had one of those rare evenings of stimulation—their two minds in tune and exploring the possibilities of the future. Michael had come away with more ideas for new projects than he could remember having in years.

He thought hard about those projects now, as if transistors could exorcise Maggie from his mind. Boats, he thought, feeling his father's vessel gently riding on a slow wave. The metering system, solar cells, wind generator—all packaged together and marketed to all sorts of vessels.

First he had to develop the direct-current metering system, then—— How could he find time to work in the electronics shop, set up the inputs and outputs and test . . .

All week Michael was too much in her thoughts, the

memory of his lips and his hands disturbing her at the most unlikely times. Once she woke dreaming of him. Several times she felt the memory sweep over her while she was in the middle of berthing boats. She got angry every time she thought of the way he had taken her in his arms against her will; yet at the same time she felt a warm, sensuous weakness at the memory of his hard, male body touching hers.

She concentrated on remembering the force he had used to kiss her, her own rage at being manhandled. This was a man who took what he wanted, and she was determined he was not going to get his way over Angus.

It was important for *Sasha* to be given a face-lift before Michael turned up again, so Maggie persisted in her plan to have the boat scrubbed and painted on the next high tide, although Angus was hesitant.

On Friday Maggie went out to buy paint and rollers, then early on Saturday morning they put *Sasha* on the tidal grid at the yacht club. Actually, Maggie did it alone in the end. Angus handled the tiller as they steamed away from his moorage under a cloudy sky, but when they turned to wind their way around the yacht club mooring floats he backed down the engine and let the tiller go.

'You better do it, Maggie.' His eyes were filled with confusion. 'I'm having trouble seeing where to go.'

'OK, I'll take over.' She hoped her distress didn't show in her voice, and she was thankful that Michael was not here to witness this sign of weakness from his father. A year or two ago Angus would have been firmly in charge, but now he made no move even to help Dixie with the docking line. Thankfully the mooring was achieved quickly and efficiently, with the help of a man passing by on shore who stopped to take the line Dixie threw ashore.

'You're in good position,' volunteered the stranger. 'Just put a little weight on the port deck to be sure she leans over this way when she sets down—then you'll be fine.'

Maggie shuddered at the thought of Angus's boat falling over when the tide went out. She and the stranger loaded on steel weights that were lying on the wharf, until the mast was slightly angled towards the pilings.

'Looks good!' said the man.

'Thanks! We really appreciate your help.' She pushed her hand back through her hair. The day was hardly started and she felt exhausted already, just thinking of the massive task ahead. 'I'm Maggie. This is Angus—and Dixie, my daughter.'

'Bob,' he volunteered. 'Dixie and I know each other from school. I'm her maths teacher.'

Dixie grimaced slightly, but when he was gone she eyed her mother and said, 'He's not married. I know that, because he was talking about moving into his apartment last week. He shares an apartment with Mr Hallsworth.'

'Forget it,' said Maggie. 'The last thing we need around here is another man.' Dixie looked shattered, and she wished she hadn't spoken so sharply, but no matter how much Maggie loved her daughter, she wouldn't go hunting for a husband just to find a father for Dixie.

Maggie got the paint and scrapers organised, then went to get the high-pressure water machine from the club manager. Angus made coffee—hot chocolate for Dixie—and they settled down to wait for the tide to go out and leave the boat sitting high on the grid. Maggie could see that Angus was starting to fret about the job of scraping and painting. Until now, he'd accepted the idea that she would help him with the job, but as the tide went out and the water around them fell, she could see him becoming more and more worried about his own inability to work.

She could have hugged Rex when he stopped on his way past to complain about his radar.

'Blinkin' thing was working last week. Don't know what's happened. I just turned it on, and there's nothing! Not even a blip!' He pushed back his messy long hair and managed to look very helpless.

This was Angus's territory and he stepped forward to ask, 'You've got one of those old Motorolas, don't you? Did you check the wave guide? Any water in the wave guide, and you won't even get a picture.'

'Yeah, but the damn thing's sealed. The guy that installed it promised me it would never leak.' Rex sounded aggrieved.

Maggie suppressed a laugh, and Angus said, 'Twenty years is a long time to keep out the water.'

Rex shrugged. 'Would you take a look at it for me, Angus? I can't find anybody uptown who'll come down to the docks for a service call.' Maggie suspected that he hadn't looked very hard.

'Go ahead,' she urged Angus. 'We'll be fine here.' She was relieved when he left. With any luck she and Dixie would finish the worst of the scraping and washing before he returned. She turned on the high-pressure water and started working.

She hadn't done this before, but she had watched others enough times, and after a while she got into the rhythm of the work, managing to sweep the hard spray of water over the boat without getting too much water in her eyes. She didn't know what she would have done without Dixie, because there seemed to be a dozen things that she needed, none of which were on Angus's boat.

The third time she sent Dixie home for something, the girl was a long time returning. Busy herself with the scrubbing and spraying, Maggie didn't even wonder where her daughter had got to.

If she had wondered, it certainly would not have occurred to her that Michael MacAvoy might have returned to Prince Rupert.

Michael had flown north in jeans this time, not a suit, although he had been forced to search his wardrobes to find the jeans. He found himself whistling as he came down the ramp to Rushbrooke floats, his eyes watching for the sight of Dixie or Maggie. All during the flight he had been trying to tell himself that he didn't care if he saw her again, and until he got to the floats he had almost succeeded in believing his own lies.

Was she married? Surely a man wouldn't leave a woman like that alone. If she were his wife, he'd . . .

He rejected the thought, angry because she was twisting herself around his mind as if she were planning to stay, and at the moment he had enough problems with handling Samantha, who seemed to have become uncharacteristically difficult.

He wasn't looking where he was going, so he was on the last finger, half-way to his father's boat before he realised *Sasha* was gone. The space was empty. He had a moment of panicky alarm, then he got his mind into gear and started thinking.

Last week Maggie had insisted that Angus was planning to paint the bottom of his boat. Angus had looked surprised, then agreed, and Michael hadn't believed a word of it. Could Dad handle a job like that? Painting and scraping, working under the boat, reaching overhead. From what he'd seen last week, Dad's balance wasn't good enough for the job. He could easily fall and hurt himself.

Damn Maggie! Somehow she had pushed Dad into this, put him at risk for the sake of winning a battle she'd impulsively decided to take on. She was determined that Dad wouldn't return to Victoria. He guessed that she was stubborn by nature, and she could easily be fighting for the sake of winning, not for Angus MacAvoy at all.

He was heading towards Maggie's door, eyes flashing and ready to give her a piece of his mind when the door flew open. A dirt-and-paint-spattered apparition came pelting out, slamming the door behind. For a second, he wasn't sure it was Dixie. Then the girl stopped abruptly in front of him, her legs spread to keep her from careening into his chest, and he saw the impish grin, the brown-green eyes flashing.

'Hi!' She shook her hair back with a gesture that made him think of Maggie. The golden curls were covered with rusty grime and she accused him, 'When did you get here? Grandpa Angus didn't tell us you're coming.'

'He didn't know. It's a surprise. Where did Dad's boat get to?' He shielded his eyes from an unexpected glare as the sun worked its way through a cloud.

'On the grid.' She gestured vaguely with an orange-spattered arm. 'Come on, I'll take you. I'm just going back. Mom wanted more soap for the sprayer.' She lifted a container to show him.

'Soap,' he mused, grinning, falling into step beside her. He had seldom seen anyone dirtier. 'I wish Heather could see you now,' he said whimsically.

'Who?' They reached the ramp and she started up,

her lithe body almost running up the steep incline.

'My sister.' Michael lengthened his stride to keep up. 'She and her daughters came to visit a few weeks back.'

'Oh.' Dixie's voice was suddenly flat. He was amused, trying to imagine the contact between this impulsive child and his restrained nieces.

'You didn't like them?'

'She called me a wharf rat,' said Dixie sulkily.

'Who? My sister?' Glancing down at Dixie, he couldn't help saying, 'If you were looking the way you do now——' but he was angry at Heather. It was one thing to walk around with her snobbish nose in the air, but to hurt a child with insults . . .

'The one with the long hair. She's got nail polish and she squints when she pretends to smile. She said 'cause I was barefoot, I was just a dirty wharf rat—I jus' came from swimming, an' I wasn't dirty!' Dixie's words were slurring in her anger. She glared at Michael.

'Jeannette.' He dropped a hand to her shoulder, half expecting she might shake it off. Then he explained, 'Jeannette hasn't got a lot of sense. I wouldn't worry about what she says. She doesn't like anyone.'

'Does she like you?' Dixie's voice was brighter now. She swung the bottle of cleaner as they walked along the side of the road.

'Not particularly. Do you want me to carry that?'

She took a firmer grip on the bottle. 'Nope. Does she really not like you? What does she say?'

He laughed. Spending time with Jeannette tended to make him feel that he was lucky not to be married and have children. The girl beside him was different, fresh and warm, everything a man might want in a daughter, but he had an uneasy feeling that if

Samantha had children they would be like his nieces. 'She doesn't say much to me. Mostly it's looks. If I'm foolish enough to try to tell a joke in her presence, she stares at me and says "Uncle Michael!" in a shocked voice, as if I'd crawled out from under a rock.'

Dixie was laughing, so he made the most of it, hoping Heather would never hear any of this. 'She has a habit of fixing me with a cold stare that always makes me wonder if I've forgotten to wash the shaving cream off my face.'

They walked together in an easy silence for a moment, then Dixie volunteered, 'I pushed her in.'

'Into the ocean?' He stopped to look at her, but she didn't seem to be joking.

'She made me so mad,' the girl explained soberly.

He could see Jeannette shaking the water off like a wet chicken, running to her mother, her ridiculous poise shattered, turning her into a real child for once. Heather—oh, lord! Heather would have been livid! He had to start laughing, thinking about Heather, remembering how virulent she had been about Maggie and the hooligan who was her daughter. He should have known that something had happened to bring on that attack from Heather.

Dixie, having realised that Michael wasn't about to berate her for her attack on his niece, had moved on to other matters. 'What should I call you?'

He wasn't ready for the question, met it with a startled stare. 'What had you thought of calling me?'

'I call Grandpa Angus Grandpa.'

'I'm not a grandpa,' he said, amused.

'No,' she agreed slowly. 'Are you married?'

'No. Are you?'

She giggled, shaking her head vigorously. 'Do you think I should call you Uncle?'

He wondered just what she had in mind. He wanted to ask about her father. It seemed a good opportunity to get some information about Maggie, but somehow he couldn't get the words out. Instead, he said, 'Why don't you call me Michael?'

She shook her head. 'Makes you sound like that lady—your sister. Michael's too stuffy. You're not like that, are you?'

'Mickey?' he suggested. She might as well. Maggie had called him Mickey when she had bitten him. Maybe it was something about the town of Prince Rupert, or the docks, but he seemed doomed to be thrown back into his youth, nicknames and all.

'How did you get so dirty, Dixie?'

'Am I dirty?' She looked down at herself, then nodded. 'Mom's pretty dirty, too. We're spraying the boat with the water machine. It cleans it all off—on to us, I guess!'

He heard the spray of the high-pressure water as they crossed the yacht club car park. There were steps going down. He could see Maggie at the bottom, standing under the boat. Out of the water, Dad's boat looked unexpectedly large.

She was holding the hose, sweeping it slowly across the hull of the boat. The whole area was engulfed in a mist, and any paint and seaweed that was forced off the boat by the spray probably found its way on to the woman standing underneath.

She was wearing a yellow rain slicker, her legs below the slicker covered with wet blue denim. She wasn't wearing boots at all, but running shoes. Perhaps she'd realised that boots would only keep the water in. He was certain that even under the slicker her clothes must be soaked.

He knew he must be crazy but, even soaking wet

and filthy, he thought she looked sexy. He tried to remember when he had looked at Sam and felt like this. As he watched, Maggie moved around to the stern of the boat where the hull swept high over her head. She held the spray nozzle awkwardly, trying to reach the underside of the transom stern while standing a couple of feet above the ground on one of the narrow beams that supported the keel of the vessel. If she didn't watch it, she'd fall right off the beam and break a leg. He started down the stairs towards her.

Maggie didn't hear him coming. The noise of the water drowned everything out. Her arms were starting to ache madly from holding the hose, but the high-pressure water was doing the job, cleaning off the old anti-fouling paint, along with the seaweed that had started to grow under the water.

She narrowed her eyes, trying to keep out the spray of water and old paint. Her eyes were stinging, probably her contact lenses complaining about the contamination. She hadn't wanted to try taking the lenses out with her hands so dirty, and in any case she had not thought to bring her lens case with her. Maybe she would send Dixie when she got back with the soap.

The water went shooting off the fibreglass hull above her, sending a wall of spray around to the other side. She couldn't see through the spray, and she hardly heard the shout of protest.

Then, when a man came walking through the mist, she pointed the water at him without realising he was there. When she realised what she had done, she jerked the spray away, sending it pounding back at herself.

'What?' she shouted.

'Turn it off!' he shouted back.

Michael. Even soaking wet, he was a thousand times more immaculate than she was. She had an impulse to ignore him and carry on spraying but, knowing he was watching, she would probably get nervous and fall off the beam. She squeezed the nozzle. The water faded abruptly to a weak trickle. Dixie came up behind Michael, dirty and grinning. 'D'ya want me to put the soap in the thing, Mom?'

'Yes, please, Dixie.'

Maggie pushed at her hair with a wet hand. Michael was taking in every detail of her appearance. She knew she was soaking wet, but her hand came away covered with flecks of old anti-fouling paint, so she must look worse than she thought.

'What are you doing here?' she asked weakly. She had planned to have this job done before he came again. With a freshly painted boat, Angus would be in a much stronger position against Michael.

He looked different today. Maybe it was the way he was dressed, but she thought he seemed less threatening, more like someone she might encounter any day on the docks.

He gestured to her hair, her clinging wet and dirty jeans. 'You're looking—ah—a little different from the last time I saw you.' She remembered the careful perfection of his sister's appearance and knew she must look like an utter slob.

'Where's Dad?' he asked, his eyes narrowing.

She grasped at the question. 'He's gone over to look at a fisherman's radar—Rex was having trouble with it, and he asked Angus to help.'

'Rex? The over-age hippie with the dog?' His eyes were still taking in the details—the scrub brush at her feet and the water machine. 'Why are you doing all this? It's no job for a woman.'

'Isn't it?' She glared at him, then the anger faded as her eyes filled with mischief. She was grinning as she handed him the nozzle and said smugly, 'I suppose it is a man's job. I'd take off that jacket if I were you. Would you like to borrow a raincoat?'

He took the nozzle, frowned, then laughed unwillingly and said, 'I guess you win that round. No, forget the raincoat. It doesn't look as if it's doing you much good. I hope there's somewhere I can have a good shower after all this?'

'The swimming pool,' she suggested. She could have offered him her shower, but the thought of Michael naked in her bathroom was more than she could handle at the moment. Trying to discomfit him, she grinned and said, 'I see your lip's getting better. It hardly shows where I bit you.'

She had thought he would be embarrassed, but he laughed again. 'Yes, Maggie,' he agreed softly. 'It's almost better. I'm thinking of having another try—but I'll change my tactics this time.'

His hair was curling wetly over his forehead. His grey eyes didn't look cool at all as they studied her. She saw him register her startled gasp, and she had a horrifying thought that he knew the wave of feeling that surged through her. Could he possibly know that a wild part of her wanted his arms around her, his lips lowering to take everything she could offer?

'Your face is like a window on your mind,' he said softly, and she felt the hot colour coming up to flush her neck and face.

Damn! Whenever she got excited, the colour flew to her face. But he wouldn't know that. He'd think it was him, and—oh, hell!

Abruptly she said, 'Hurry with the water. We've got to get two coats of anti-fouling on before the tide comes back in. There isn't any time to waste.'

She'd forgotten Dixie's presence, but her daughter hadn't missed a word of their exchange. Before Michael could get the water started spraying against the hull, Dixie was asking, 'Why did my mom bite you?'

Maggie fled quickly, before either of them could see her flaming face. Let Michael deal with that one. He'd earned it. She went topsides. High above Michael she could hear the water going, could look down and see the top of his head, his hair wet and curling, his shoulders broad and strong. Last weekend, she had thought it was a victory when he had gone home without Angus.

She wished he had stayed in Victoria. Angus needed looking after, but she and Dixie would do that. They were his family now, and this was where Angus wanted to be.

Maggie kept remembering Michael's arms around her, his lips on hers. No, she didn't want that! If she was going to let a man take her in his arms, kiss her lips, let it be someone like Darryl—an attractive friend who would not tangle her insides into knots. Michael was a different matter, he saw too much. Angus was right—Michael made plans, then he got what he wanted. He hadn't forgotten about them, or given up. He'd just changed his tactics and come back.

Well, if he thought charming her would give him a victory over Angus, he'd soon learn otherwise! She would change *her* tactics, too. By the time this weekend was over, Michael would have to admit that Angus had a family here, that he was getting the best of care, and that he was happy.

He might be easier to handle if she thought of him as Mickey, not Michael. He was Angus's son, and there must have been a time when Angus had ruled him, even spanked him for being naughty. She grinned at the thought of Michael MacAvoy receiving a spanking. Then she got out the paint and the rollers, and started painting the bow where the water had already dried.

'I'm going to look as disreputable as the two of you by the time I'm done,' Michael said wryly when he finished spraying and took up his roller.

'You already do,' said Maggie happily. 'You don't look anything at all like the respectable man who came down to the docks last week.'

He didn't act like it, either. He seemed to be enjoying the whole thing—water and dirt and paint. He wasn't very good with the roller at first, but Maggie didn't have a chance to feel smug about her own skill. He might not have spent much of his life painting, but by the time an hour had gone by, he was spreading on paint like a pro.

When they were almost finished the first coat, Dixie jumped down off one of the beams and landed on the edge of the paint tray. Maggie turned swiftly at the noise.

'Dixie! Are you all right? You—oh! Look at you!' The girl was covered in orange-red paint from her feet to her chest.

'Jeepers!' said Dixie, and Michael started to laugh.

Maggie swung on him. 'This isn't funny! Look at her!'

He said, grinning, 'Dixie, if you had a picture of yourself like this, you could use it to shock Jeannette right into the water again.

Dixie giggled. 'Mom, it's only my old trousers, an' I didn't like this shirt anyway.'

Maggie said grimly, 'You may not have liked it, but you aren't the one paying for your new clothes!'

Michael's voice dropped to a gentle murmur. 'You didn't really expect that she was going to be able to wear those things again after this, did you?'

His eyes seemed to look right past her tense anger. She found herself relaxing, looking at her daughter again, unable to resist a smile at the sight. 'You'd better go back and change, hadn't you, honey?'

Mother and daughter giggled at each other, then Dixie took off towards Rushbrooke, calling, 'I'll be right back!'

Maggie felt a sudden surge of warmth as she met Michael's eyes again. She said defensively, 'I suppose you think I was being silly, getting angry about that.'

'Maggie, if my sister had been in your place, she would have had us all saying penance for months—No, I take that back. Heather would never—I can't imagine anything that would induce her to clean up the bottom of a boat.' He picked up the overturned paint tray and poured more paint into it. Then he was painting the stern with his roller, his back to her.

Maggie glanced down at herself and grimaced. Heaven knew what her face looked like, and her hair was a disaster! Last week he might have thought she was attractive, but even a crazy man would run from her if he saw her now.

She was suddenly afraid that he would turn and catch her thoughts. What had he said? That her face was like a window on her mind? If he saw her now, he would know exactly what she was thinking. Why should the sight of this wet, paint-spattered man arouse her so much? The heat surged as she tried frantically to think of something else. What had they been talking about?

'Your sister,' she said abruptly. 'Mrs Steinworth.'

'Heather,' corrected Michael, rolling the paint on smoothly over his head, not noticing the faint spatter of orange that was covering his face. 'She probably didn't make a very good impression.'

'Immaculate,' said Maggie, remembering how the woman had glared as she surveyed Maggie's old jeans and sneakers.

Michael said wryly, 'Right now—the last few years—she's got into a bad phase. She has the idea that the most important thing is being invited to the right places, having the right friends.'

'Oh.' Maggie frowned. She picked up the other roller and carefully rolled it through the paint in the tray. She rolled paint over the first coat. 'It's a good thing this stuff dries fast, or we'd never get two coats on during one tide. The water's already coming close.'

He was working steadily with the roller, but his voice sounded disapproving as he asked, 'Why did you get this colour?'

'It's the copper that makes it red, and copper's the active ingredient that keeps the growth off the boat.' There were other colours of anti-fouling paint, but they were more expensive, and she had wanted to save Angus whatever money she could.

She was covering large areas with the roller. Michael was silent, but she was a talkative girl, so she chattered on, 'We'll be done before Dixie gets back. That'll save her getting another set of clothes covered in paint.'

Michael finally asked, 'Speaking of which, don't you think Dad should be back by now?' She could see his feet as he moved position to reach the extreme back of the boat. Those expensive leather shoes would never be the same again.

'I expected Rex would keep him for quite a while,'

she said.

'Looking at a radar?' He sounded dissatisfied, perhaps worried. 'There's not much he can do without test equipment.'

Maggie stepped on to a plank spanning two of the beams. 'He said something about a wave guide. Angus thought there might be water in it. It sounded like the kind of thing that would take a while.'

'It doesn't make much sense, his going off like that while his boat's on the grid.'

She made a face at him, but he couldn't see. There really wasn't much point in trying to fool him. She said quietly, daring him to make something of it, 'I encouraged him to go. If he works on Rex's radar, he'll feel good about that, feel useful. I know Rex will keep him as long as he can, asking about more than the radar. Nothing electric ever works right on Rex's boat, and he's always short of money. He'll get all the free advice he can from Angus and—if your dad stayed here——' She took a deep breath, admitted, 'There's too much in this job that he can't do any more. I wanted to get it done without making him feel like——' She stopped abruptly. Her roller was still as she listened for his response, but he was silent. She saw his feet move, knew he was coming around to her end of the boat.

'You don't have to come here,' she said breathlessly. 'I can hear you from the other end.'

'I wanted to see what you were thinking,' he said simply. He held her eyes for long seconds. The cool grey of his had deepened to a warm blue. He said gently, 'You're a nice woman, Maggie,' as if the discovery surprised him.

CHAPTER FOUR

IT WAS a big tide and the water came in fast. By the time Dixie came back with Angus in tow, the sea had already risen to the curve of the bilge. Maggie and Michael washed as well as they could in the yacht club washroom while Angus and Dixie walked to town and brought back a bag filled with plastic containers of milk, and another over-flowing with fresh doughnuts.

Then they stood around on the platform outside the boat, eating and watching the water, as if they could make the tide come in more quickly.

'We're done,' said Maggie happily. 'Doesn't she look nice, Angus?'

'Sparkling,' he agreed with a smile. He had lost his earlier tension. Even the sight of his son working on the boat didn't seem to disturb him. 'Thanks, Maggie—and you, too, Dixie.'

'And Mickey,' mumbled Dixie as she stuffed another doughnut into her wide mouth. She looked better now, cleaner, although her face was decorated by the occasional spot of orange.

'And Mickey,' agreed Angus. 'All of you. I couldn't have done it myself.'

Maggie glanced swiftly at Michael, and was relieved that he didn't seem to have pounced on Angus's admission. He seemed most interested in the milk he was drinking, but after a long swallow he said, 'It's been fun, but next time why don't you put it into a yard to have it done? Isn't there a shipyard up here?'

'A couple of them,' said Maggie. 'But it's expensive.'

Michael said wryly, 'Not that expensive.'

Angus shook his head, and said simply, 'I just never thought of it.'

Maggie had always assumed that Angus had very little income, but neither he nor Michael seemed to feel that money should be an obstacle. His grey hair blew in the breeze as he said slowly, 'Haven't been thinking much about looking after the boat the last couple of years, but—— I'd like to take you all out to dinner.' He looked at Maggie and Mickey, a grin growing on his face. 'First, maybe you should have a shower, though.'

'I'll vote for that,' agreed Michael. 'The shower, and the dinner. Somewhere that serves good food and lots of it! How'd you make out with the radar, Dad?'

'Water in the wave guide,' said Angus. 'We got it working.' He was leaning against the rail as if he were a little tired, but he looked happy and Maggie said a silent thank-you to Michael for being the person he was today, warm and approving.

When the water was high enough, Angus let Maggie take the helm. He seemed content to sit in the cockpit and watch her manoeuvre the sail-boat through the narrow exit to the harbour, until Dixie came running back from the foredeck where she had been standing with Michael and said eagerly, 'Grandpa Angus, let's have a game of draughts.'

That left Maggie and Michael alone in the cockpit, and she didn't protest when he took the tiller from her, saying, 'You're tired. Curl up in the corner there and rest.' He called down through the companionway, 'Dixie! Bring up a cushion for your mother, would you?' And, before Maggie knew it, she was settled back in the corner, leaning against a big, soft cushion, her eyes closing.

She let the gentle motion of the boat overwhelm her like a trance. Drifting, almost dizzy, it seemed she was alone in the world, in a place where all the tensions drifted away. When her eyes opened and took in Michael, he seemed to belong there.

'Are we almost there?' Dazed from sleep, she smiled a warm smile that took his breath away. She pushed back her short curls and stretched. 'I feel so lazy, I don't want to move.'

'Don't,' he urged. His smile was relaxed and boyish, miles from the Michael she had seen the week before. She decided that she liked him, that he was a nice man who wasn't going to do any harm to his father. He said, 'Just relax where you are. You're in no hurry to get back, are you?'

'Where are we?' She twisted to look out, saw that he had taken them across the harbour.

He said, 'It's such a nice day, and I didn't think there was any hurry.'

'There isn't,' she agreed, sinking back against the cushion. She had taken the rain-jacket off hours ago, and the sun had dried her clothes. 'Dixie?' she asked.

'Downstairs with Dad. Still playing the draughts championship.' He narrowed his eyes to look across the harbour. The cloud cover had disappeared, leaving only a few fluffy white clouds in a deep blue sky.

He lifted one leg up on to the cockpit seat and leaned back into the corner by the tiller. His hand controlled their course lazily, his eyes half closed as he looked around at the water and the mountains. 'A tie,' he told her, a slight smile still on his lips. 'They've both got two games, and they're going for the best out of seven.' He lifted a paint-spattered hand to shield his eyes from the sun. 'God, Maggie! This is a beautiful place!'

'When the sun shines,' she agreed. 'The green mountains and the blue sky, the water. I guess that's why so many of us stay here, put up with all the rain.'

'What about you, Maggie? Why are you here?'

She shrugged, letting her eyes close again. She wished the day could go on for ever, this feeling of warm peace.

'What keeps you here?' he asked again, his voice easy, not demanding.

She shifted to a more comfortable position. Soon she would get up and get busy, but until then she wanted to savour this rare feeling of peace. She said to Michael, 'It's my place.' From the beginning she had felt she belonged here. After the turmoil of her marriage, it had been as if the water gave her control of her life again.

'You don't wear a wedding ring. Does that mean you're not married?' His voice hadn't changed, but when her eyelids jerked open she saw that he had lost the sleepy look. For a minute he was seeing right into her, then she managed to tear her gaze away from his. She picked up the cushion, holding it in front of herself as she got up, as if it were a barrier.

'No, I'm not married,' she agreed tightly. 'I'm going down to watch that draughts match. You seem to have everything under control up here.'

When she got below, she realised from the startled look Angus gave her that she had been almost running. Crazy woman! Running from a little question like that. Are you married? No, damn it! She wasn't married. Never again! She could have said, 'I'm divorced.' But then he might have asked about Dick. He didn't seem to hesitate to ask questions, and with his eyes on her she might have started answering.

Angus was still watching her. She knew he could hear the high, almost frantic note in her voice as she explained, 'He asks too many questions.'

She stepped into the galley and moved a couple of dirty glasses. Angus turned back to the draughts game and let her fuss around with the dishes as if she were performing some purpose there. What must Michael think? She had run away as if the question terrified her, yet there was Dixie as evidence that Maggie was no virginal maiden. She didn't wear a wedding ring, so now he would probably think Dixie was illegitimate.

Well, let him! Why should it bother her? These days, it was not unusual for a woman to have a child alone. It didn't matter, anyway. He would be gone in a couple of days. Tomorow, probably. Meanwhile, she would freeze him out. He had softened her today, getting into the dirt and fun of doing the boat's bottom; but he was a dangerous man to go soft on. The boyish innocence of his face must not make her forget the times those grey eyes went right through her.

Michael got what he wanted, planned it and got it. Right now he wanted Angus back on dry land, in Victoria. Maggie was the main obstacle, and maybe knowing the enemy gave him some sort of power over her. Yes, that was why he was asking questions, but he wasn't going to beat her that way. She would be cool now, cool and unresponsive and polite. She practised being cool, down in the galley out of his sight. She practised calling him Mickey in her mind, because she knew that disconcerted him.

'Coming in to dock!' Despite her mental brain-washing, she wasn't ready for his voice calling down to her. She had to take a deep breath to get herself armoured before she ran up on deck, a meaningless smile firmly in place for his benefit.

She got the lines in place for docking with an efficiency that might have been more impressive if Dixie hadn't been helping with such enthusiasm. It all seemed to be wasted on Michael. He was concentrating on bringing the boat into the small space beside her barge, and she had to admit he did a good job of it, coming alongside neatly without a lot of fuss and roaring of the engine.

Maggie left Michael alone to figure out the tying-up process. 'I'll take a shower,' she told Angus. 'Then maybe I'll be fit to be seen with.'

It was amazing what soap and water could do for her morale. It took a lot of scrubbing, but once she had the paint out of her hair, and off her skin, she felt ready for anything. Thank goodness for Jan and her endless supply of quality rummage-sale clothes! Maggie dug through her friend's latest gift box of treasures and found a beautiful hand-embroidered blouse and a swirling, wrap-around skirt that made her feel feminine and almost elegant once she had slipped into matching high-heeled sandals.

He wasn't going to be able to compare her unfavourably with his fancy sister tonight. She smiled and decided to relent and invite Michael to shower at her place, but when she came out of the bedroom she shared with Dixie, clean and dressed to kill, Angus and Dixie were alone in the living-room.

'Where's Mickey?' she asked, remembering that she wasn't going to call him Michael.

'Showering,' said Angus.

'But your shower's not working.'

'Tis now!' said Dixie smugly as she headed for the shower herself. 'Mickey fixed it.'

So even Angus's temperamental shower had bent to that man's will. She felt a surge of irritation when he appeared in a smoothly tailored casual suit. Naturally, with that bloody efficiency, he had brought a full change of clothes. She had expected that he would have to return home in paint-covered jeans and a jacket that would never be the same again. Now she had to content herself with the knowledge that he would have to buy a new pair of shoes after this weekend.

They went to Smiles Café for dinner, and asked for a table looking out over the harbour. It was a gay meal, filled with laughter and good food, although Maggie avoided Michael's eyes until Michael got Angus talking about his travels on the boat. Then Maggie was so fascinated at the places the old man had travelled to before he came to Prince Rupert that she forgot her vow not to be friendly with Michael.

'Did you go on any of these trips, Michael?' Maggie had been watching him, and was surprised to realise that he too was affected by the romance of his father's travels.

'Just a couple of weeks one summer.' For a second she forgot her resolve and met his eyes with warm curiosity, then she remembered and concentrated intently on her food.

Angus said, 'Mickey was too busy building his empire. He had no time for fun.'

'What empire?' asked the irrepressible Dixie.

'Work,' Michael told her with a smile. Maggie couldn't imagine how she had ever thought his eyes were cold. 'Business. Dad's right. It wouldn't have hurt me to take a little time away from it.' He turned to Maggie impulsively. 'Maggie, why don't we go dancing tonight?'

Her eyes lit for a second, meeting his. Then she remembered who he was, what he wanted. She concentrated on the plate in front of her and and said carefully, 'No, thanks, Michael. I'll pass.'

She glanced up and was startled by a flash of hot anger in his eyes. Along his cheekbone, a muscle jerked, then relaxed as Angus said, 'Come on, Maggie. You don't get out often enough—and you love dancing.'

'I'm not dressed for it,' she said weakly, avoiding Michael's eyes.

'You're gorgeous,' said Michael, startling her eyes back to his. She looked for some sign that he was playing games with her, but all she could see was admiration, as if he really thought she were a beautiful woman. 'We'll go when we finish dinner,' he said decisively.

His eyes were telling her that he wanted to kiss her again. She tried not to let him see the weak trembling that overcame her when she thought of his kiss. She said breathlessly, 'Michael, I don't have a babysitter.'

Dixie sat up straight. 'I don't need a babysitter, Mom! I'm old enough, and besides—don't you remember? Carol wants me to sleep over.'

Maggie looked doubtful. Her daughter added swiftly, 'We're working on our science project together.'

'Come on,' Michael said softly.

She met his eyes, then her gaze dropped to the faint, dark line of a scar on his lip. His mouth twitched in the beginnings of a smile and she flushed, remembering how his hands had felt through the back of her dress.

He said persuasively, 'I promise to behave.'

Dixie giggled at the notion that grown-ups might not behave, and Maggie said grimly, 'You'd better.'

Dixie left the café first, eating her dessert quickly while the adults relaxed over coffee, then dashing off to get her things and go to Carol's for the night. 'Don't worry about her,' said Angus as Dixie rushed away.

Maggie frowned. 'I do. She's too mature for her age, and she gets her way so easily with me. I think she's got me taped.'

'She's a good kid,' said Michael. 'If she were mine, I'd be proud of her.'

Maggie met his eyes with a trace of defiance. 'I *am* proud of her, but she's no angel.' She took a deep breath before she admitted, 'She got mad at your niece and shoved her into the water. She—you're laughing!'

'I know about that. Dixie told me. I'd have loved to be there!'

Angus snorted. 'No, you wouldn't. Heather made everyone's life hell. I had words with her over it, and she didn't take very well to having her father telling her off at her age.'

Maggie shook her head at Michael, saying flatly, 'Dixie was wrong to do it. She has a terrible temper sometimes.' Michael touched the mark on his lip and Maggie said quickly, 'I have a temper, too.'

'I had noticed,' he murmured.

Maggie didn't remember consenting to go out with Michael, but it seemed she was going. Michael called a taxi when they had finished their coffee. He held the passenger door for Maggie and Angus to get in, then gave the driver instructions to stop at Rushbrooke for Angus.

'Why don't you come with us?' Maggie suggested to Angus as the taxi drove the short distance to the floats.

He shook his head. 'Maggie, I'm tired. I'm going to

sit out in the cockpit and have a beer, then I'm going to bed for a long sleep. Don't make a lot of noise when you come in, Mickey!'

'I'll be quiet,' his son promised, laughing. As they drove away, he said to Maggie, 'I half expect him to tell me I'd better be in by midnight or I'll be grounded.'

'Was he a stern father?' She tried to imagine Angus being stern, and she couldn't.

'Not often,' admitted Michael as the taxi turned up the hill towards the downtown area. 'And when he was, I deserved it. Actually, I was spoiled rotten. I got everything I wanted.'

Maggie grinned, trying to imagine him in a losing battle. 'Angus says you still do.'

'Does he?' He was frowning, not pleased by his father's evaluation. When he frowned, the mark her teeth had made showed clearly on his lip. At least that was one battle he had lost!

Maggie said softly, watching his reaction, 'He says you decide what you want, and make plans to get it. And your plans work.'

The taxi pulled up outside the nightclub. Michael reached for his wallet to pay the driver, then held the door for her as she climbed out. When she stood on the pavement, she was close enough to smell the spicy scent of his aftershave. Her hands clenched at her sides, resisting a crazy urge to touch his face.

'Is there anything wrong with that?' he asked, trapping her with cold, grey eyes.

Confused, she asked, 'What are you talking about?'

'About going for the things I want. I'm just wondering why that should be a bad thing.' He slid her hand inside his arm and turned towards the doors of the nightclub.

'I—it depends.' With her high heels, she didn't feel quite so dwarfed by him. She let her hand stay where he'd put it, deciding that pulling it away would only reveal her inner turmoil.

'Depends on what?' he demanded as he held the door.

'On what you want. How you go about getting it.' She felt a sudden surge of anger giving her strength. 'In my experience you have a habit of grabbing for things that aren't yours.'

'A moment of insanity,' he said softly as they were seated at a small table. A cocktail waitress came and took their orders, then he told her quietly, 'You were very beautiful that night—you're a very desirable woman, Maggie, and last Saturday I was not in my right mind. I'd have apologised before this, but it seemed to me that you'd inflicted more than adequate punishment on me for my transgressions.'

He was smiling now, but she remembered his howl of agony as her teeth sank into his lip. She giggled, then sobered. 'I've never done anything like that to anyone before in my life. I was furious!'

'That I had guessed,' he said wryly.

'You deserved it,' she added fiercely.

'Admitted,' he said, reaching across the table for her hand. He turned her palm up and stared at it, his thumb massaging gently. 'Next time——'

'There won't be a next time!' She tugged her hand away. Could he know that she had dreams of his touching her?

When the music started, she found herself entrusting her hand to his, being led out on to the floor and into his arms. He wasn't an expert dancer, but a comfortable one, bringing her close into his arms and moving slowly and rhythmically with her to the music.

'There will be a next time, Maggie,' he promised her, his voice low and filled with meaning as he guided her around another couple.

She felt dizzy, drowning, couldn't stop her body from resting close against his, as if in surrender. His hands were firm on her back, the fingers moving slightly, caressing through the fabric of her blouse. She melted closer, letting him lead her, not caring where their steps took them. Next time, he had said.

It would be tonight, when he took her home. His lips would cover hers, taking what she had refused to give last Saturday. She felt her own response surging through her, a wave of heat that left her trembling, painfully aware of his touch, his closeness. She tensed, frightened by her own response. This was just a dance, for heaven's sake! How many men had she danced with? It had never been like this.

It wasn't the man. He was attractive, and of course she was attracted, but it must be that he had turned up at a bad time for her. There had been Dick's letter, and that must have upset her more than she knew. Dick wanting her back, and this wild, passionate urge for a man who was almost a stranger. Yes, that must be it. Just a way of escaping from Dick.

If she had an affair with Michael, might that not counter the crazy guilt that made her think she should say yes when Dick stood in front of her, begging her to come back? Michael would be safe. Like Darryl, he fitted the requirements. Here today, gone tomorrow.

Tomorrow he would go back to Victoria. Back to—God! What was she doing? What kind of man was he, playing with her, dancing and touching and teasing, his eyes telling her he wanted her? What about the woman who waited for him, who lived with him?

She said suddenly, bitterly. 'Aren't you forgetting something, Mickey?' She pulled away, stiff in his arms, looking up accusingly. 'What about your woman? Is this your usual pattern? Playing around, cheating on her? Does she know this is how you behave when you're not with her?'

His eyes widened as if he had forgotten about Sam, then his fingers dug into the flesh at her back. He said tightly, 'Maggie, I'm not——'

'Angus said you're living with her. Her name is Samantha and you've been living with her for a year.' She took a deep breath, then added, 'Angus doesn't like her.' He had stopped moving, his eyes holding hers. Her voice became very sombre, very earnest. 'Michael, I don't go out with married men, or even——'

He drew her closer, his feet moving again to the music. She felt herself moving to his guidance, as if she had no will of her own. He said, 'Maggie, I'm not married. Sam and I aren't—we're not in love with each other.'

Michael felt panicked at the sound of his own words. He had not intended this when he'd flown north this morning. He knew that his relationship with Sam was on the verge of collapse, but he wasn't normally the kind of man who two-timed a woman. Even for a woman like Maggie. Goodness knew he wanted her, but she frightened him in a way Sam never had. She was hot and fiery, capable of turning his ordered life upside-down.

He was relieved when she said quickly, 'I don't want to get involved with anyone. Especially——'

His fingers covered her lips, stopping the low-voiced flow of half-angry words. 'An evening's dancing?' he said softly. 'I'd enjoy it, and so would you. Then later, when I see you home. I'd like to kiss you again.' She said nothing, but her body was softly pressed against his and he could feel her tremble. 'You'll give me one evening, won't you, Maggie? One evening, and tomorrow I'll be gone?'

The silence grew. She was glad of her face pressed against his shoulder, his arms around her for support. He couldn't see her face, and she couldn't answer. She felt a panic-stricken eagerness that frightened her. She took refuge in silence. Then, when the music quickened, she slipped away from him, twisting her body to the rhythm, dancing without touching. His body seemed in tune with every movement hers made. Separated by several feet of dance-floor, nevertheless they seemed locked together by the music and their eyes as they danced in the dimly lit nightclub.

The next selection was even wilder, forcing them to move fast and furiously to keep up with it. By the time the band's frenzy faded to silence, both Maggie and Michael were laughing and exhausted.

'Enough!' He caught her hand. 'We'll sit this one out.' He slipped his arm around her shoulders, leading her back to the table where she collapsed.

'I'm too old for this,' she panted as she picked up her drink to take a large gulp of the cool liquid.

'Gorgeous old lady!' He dropped down across from her, lifted his own glass in a silent toast to her.

'I'm twenty-nine.' She didn't know why she wanted to tell him that. She licked her lips self-consciously.

'You look younger.' His eyes deepened suddenly, taking her unawares. 'You look far too young to have a daughter the size of Dixie.'

'She's ten,' Maggie said abruptly. 'Almost eleven.'

'So you were eighteen? Or seventeen?' His voice made no judgements, but she thought she could read his mind.

'I was married.' Her voice rose, her cheeks flushed. 'I know what you've been thinking, that Dixie—that I wasn't married, that I must have——'

His hand covered hers, tightening. 'Maggie, stop it!' His sharp voice silenced her. She stared at him, her eyes wide and vulnerable.

'Michael—Mickey, I don't want to talk about it.'

'I know you don't.' His thumb caressed the back of her hand. 'Maggie, I—I hate to think of you married at seventeen! What in hell were your parents thinking of to let you get married at that age? You were just a child. Surely your father——'

She pulled her hand away. 'A seventeen-year-old girl is no child! For heaven's sake, Michael! Dixie's just turning eleven, and look at her. She's already starting to develop into a woman. By the time she's seventeen, she'll be giving me all the trouble I gave my parents.'

He had her hand again. She didn't try to pull it away. She said, 'I was a pretty rebellious teenager,' and he grinned.

'Somehow I can believe that.'

She pushed her hair back. Earlier she had brushed it to a smooth, controlled halo, but it had sprung into its usual tumbled mass of glowing curls. 'I love my father. We've always been close—until I was in my teens and started dating. Then he seemed to get—— He was very authoritarian, and at the time I thought he was terribly unfair. I felt that he kept me so penned down. I couldn't go to any parties unless he knew the parents, and knew they were home and——' She laughed ruefully. 'It sounds silly, but it was embarrassing sometimes. He'd phone up and check. He was always worried about me, never trusted the boys I went out with.'

Michael tried to imagine himself as father to an older Dixie, sitting home waiting for her to come home. He said carefully, 'Maggie, I can't really blame him. Teenage boys do have a one-track mind.'

'Men don't?' she retorted swiftly.

'Oh, yes,' he admitted with a laugh. 'But twenty-nine-year-old women can hold their own.'

She grinned. 'Hmm. I doubt my father would concede that, even now. When I was in my teens, it was—— Oh, you wouldn't have believed our house! The rules and the regulations and the fighting! It was one long battle—me fighting for freedom! You'd have thought I was one of the oppressed of the world, the way I fought him.

'My mother tried to stay out of the battle. Sometimes she tried to get me to tame down a bit, and sometimes she tried softening him—at least, I think she did. She believed in presenting a united front, but behind the scenes I do think she tried to make him ease up on his restrictions. Michael, when I think about Dixie, it really makes me shudder. She's like me in a lot of ways, and I'm terrified that we'll end up battling like that when she gets a little older. I——'

She stopped abruptly, pulling her hand away from his. What was she doing, confiding her worries about Dixie and her own wild adolescence? Only a few hours ago this man had been an enemy.

'Maggie——'

'I don't usually ramble on like this. Sorry.' She was afraid to look at his face. She looked around desperately, her fingers playing nervously with her glass. 'See that fellow over there? The one with the beard? He came in yesterday. He's captain of a big boat from San Francisco. You should see——'

Michael didn't even look. 'I want to hear the rest of it, Maggie. With a strict father and someone as emotional as you, I'm sure the fireworks were spectacular.'

'I'm not emotional,' she denied. 'I just—oh, damn it, Michael! Don't laugh!'

'All right,' he agreed, still smiling. 'Come and dance with me again, then.' He stood up and held out his hand for her, as if they danced together always.

'I don't think——'

'Don't think,' he urged as he took her hand and drew her up to him. When he had her close in his arms on the dance-floor, he murmured, 'Just feel, Maggie. Tell me how the young Maggie met the fair knight who freed her.'

He knew too much. Could he really see how it had been, without knowing her or Dick? 'I graduated when I was seventeen, went to university.'

His arms tightened around her. 'And tasted freedom?'

She nodded, and he felt the movement on his shoulder. 'It went to my head. The parties and the dancing.' Dick had courted her, made her feel beautiful and exciting. The heady excitement had intoxicated her.

'Then?' He swung her around another couple. He looked down at her, his eyes only inches from hers. For a moment she thought his lips would move closer to cover hers. His low voice said, 'I'm glad the band seems to be into slow music at the moment. This is nice.' His arm tightened on her waist and she let her eyes close as her head found a place against his shoulder.

She tried to remember how she had felt at first when she had met Dick. He had been laying claim on her, and she had felt special, treasured, a grown-up woman who had her own man. She tried to remember if she had felt the desire for marriage and children. She murmured, 'Everything fell apart when I got my first term's marks. I'd done a lot more playing than working, and it showed in my marks.'

'And your father reacted?' Michael guessed.

'When I got back from classes one day, he was there waiting. He told me to get upstairs and pack my bags. He was taking me home the next morning.' Mostly, she remembered the humiliation of knowing her friends were watching.

'That was a mistake,' decided Michael.

Maggie giggled. Michael shifted, and somehow she found both her arms curved up around his neck. 'I suppose you'd have done it differently?'

'It's a tricky one, I admit.' He drew her even closer, so that her breasts were crushed againt his chest, her skirt floating around his legs. 'I think I'd have tried to avoid a direct confrontation. It's not the way to——' He almost said 'handle you,' but replaced it with, 'handle the situation.'

'Well, it didn't work very well. Dad towed me out to dinner, and I sat listening to him lay down the law. I thought the world had ended.'

'So you got married?'

She nodded. 'Crazy, when you think of it, isn't it? Trying to get free of an overbearing father, running straight to another man for protection.'

The music swelled in volume. She became aware that her fingers were caressing the back of his neck, stroking the fine hairs that grew there. She pulled her arm back so that it rested on the fabric of his suit jacket. 'So we eloped. That's enough,' she said, keeping her voice very light. 'We'll skip the rest of my life story.'

She felt his eyes on her and stirred in his arms. Then, somehow, her hand crept back up the skin at the back of his neck. Her fingers caressed, the sensation sending a shudder of desire through her, the music pulsing in her veins.

CHAPTER FIVE

MICHAEL bent down to help Maggie out of the taxi, his hand gentle yet firm on hers. When she was standing beside him, he slipped an arm around her waist to hold her close while he paid the driver. Then the taxi drove away, leaving them alone under a moonlit sky.

They had been wrapped in magic all evening. Sometimes she had hardly heard the words he said, her eyes were so busy taking in the sight of him. She could feel his thoughts and he could read everything in her eyes. She was content to let his arm guide her away from the car park as the taxi drove away. He stopped at the pier and they stood, together, sharing the enchantment of a moonlit harbour, boats and masts in silhouette against a grey-black sky.

He turned her to face him, took her face in his hands, his eyes staring deeply into hers. She watched his lips moving closer, saw them part in anticipation just before they touched hers. She felt weakness flowing in her veins, felt herself leaning against his firmness for support.

'Michael . . .' Her whisper hardly moved the air between them. She melted towards him. Her arms slipped up to possess his shoulders, his neck. Her eager fingers moved through the crisp curls of his hair.

Michael touched her gently, exploring. She could feel his heart thundering against her as his kiss deepened towards possession. She clung tightly. His lips were firm, his tongue exploring the softness of her mouth, his hands hard and exciting along the curves of her back. Her fingers tightened in his hair, her arms tensing, drawing his head closer, drawing herself tautly against him, her breasts swelling as they pressed against his muscular chest.

His hands explored the curve of her hips, the round-ness of her firm buttocks. They firmed and drew her close, until she gasped at the erotic sensation of Michael close to her.

'Maggie,' he groaned. 'Oh, Maggie!'

His lips were hot on her mouth, then possessing the soft skin of her throat. One hand moved up to claim the swollen fullness of her breast and she was helpless, lost in a heated tide of weakness and desire that flooded over her. His fingers fumbled, slipped through the gap where a button had opened, touched warm, aching flesh, bringing a formless sound from her throat.

'Maggie,' his voice came low and warm at her ear. 'I want to be with you, Maggie.' She could hear his voice all through her, a low growl that throbbed in her veins.

Her eyes half opened, seeing his face, the eyes im-penetrable in the dark. In the moonlight she could hardly see, but she could feel his need and her own heated response urging her to surrender her woman's body to him. Her lips parted, her breath quickening as his mouth moved over hers.

Long, drugged moments later she clung to him as his lips left hers, his body straightening. 'Someone coming,' he mumbled, his lips hovering over the soft flesh under her jaw, enjoying the taste of her skin, the feel of her trembling to his touch.

She could hear it now. Footsteps below, then the sound of someone walking up the ramp. She let Michael lead the way, let her arm find its own place, slipped around his waist under his suit jacket. They passed the man at the top of the ramp, then he was gone and they were walking down together, alone again.

'Steep!' gasped Maggie as her high heels threw her off balance on the steep ramp. Then Michael's arm was lifting her and they swept down the ramp side by side, her feet hardly touching, her laughter warm in the dark.

At the bottom he swept her into his arms again. She went eagerly, raising her lips to his, giving herself to his kiss before his lips asked. She felt him trembling, or was it herself?

'You're dynamite, lady!' he whispered against her throat.

'Maybe it's you,' she said on a gasp. She slipped her arms around his neck again, her fingers caressing as they drew him closer. His hands moved sensuously across her back as she added breathlessly, 'I've never felt quite like this before!'

'Maggie, I— Let's go somewhere we can be alone.' He held her rigidly as a spasm of desire overwhelmed him.

She didn't want to step away from him, even the little way that was required for walking side by side. She knew he felt the same need, because he held her close at his side as they went slowly along the wharf in the darkness. They were turning on to the last finger when she realised, 'Dixie! Oh, Michael, we can't—'

He caught her close again, his lips pressing a quick, heated kiss against hers. 'Dixie's out. Remember? She's sleeping over at a friend's.'

'Carol's.' Maggie trembled with the realisation of how badly she wanted to be with this man. In a moment they would open her door, step inside, and she could give herself up to his touch, his kisses and delightful caresses. Along with the shuddering desire, she felt a sudden, trembling fear. It had been so long since she had been this close to a man. 'Michael, I——'

His hands were suddenly soft on her face, his voice very gentle. 'It's all right, sweetheart.' His lips brushed hers softly. 'It'll be all right.'

She trembled from his touch, then whispered, 'I——'

'Shh, sweetheart.' His hands were feather-light, shaping her cheekbones, his thumbs gently closing her eyes.

She shook her head, the words trembling on her lips. 'Michael, last week—when you—when Darryl and I came home, you—you said I was a tease.' She sucked in an unsteady breath. 'It's true. I——Well, I'm used to coming home, and there's no question of anyone coming in. Dixie's always there.'

'Protecting you?' he suggested, covering her lips again, finding them still soft and responsive to his touch. 'Are you trying to tell me you don't want me to come in tonight?'

She shivered. He took her lips with his, taking her mouth in a deep kiss, drawing a shuddering response from her. His hands travelled over the curves of her shoulders, cupped one full breast and felt the hard rigidity of her erect nipple, even through the fabric.

He knew how difficult he was making it for her to push him away, knew it was probably an unfair tactic, but he needed her so badly, he hardly even thought of stopping. His thumb and forefinger found her nipple through the blouse and bra as his lips reluctantly left hers. 'If you want to fight me off,' he said softly, 'there's no need to bite.' He bent and used his lips to nip gently at the sensitive peak his fingers held, his mouth returning to hers to take the soft gasp from her lips. Maggie . . . He drank in the intoxicating taste of her, willing her to want him.

'I don't want to fight you off,' she said shakily. She wanted his hands on her, his lips touching her everywhere. She wanted to touch him, too, to feel him gasp and groan. With a nervous excitement, she acknowledged to herself that she wanted to make him tremble as no woman ever had done before. He was guiding her steps towards her barge, and she fumbled blindly for her key in her bag, acknowledging to herself that she wanted nothing more than his touch on her.

'Maggie, there's a light on in the living-room.'

'I probably left it on.' Her fingers found the key and drew it out. 'I'm always forgetting to turn lights off. That's why Angus thought of putting in solar cells for me. I kept running my batteries flat.' She handed him the key, knowing that her trembling fingers would fumble the job of unlocking her door.

He took it, staring down at the small piece of metal in his hand. Then he looked at her, as if he were asking her something, although there were no words and it was too dark for eyes to talk. This was her chance to make some nervous excuse and escape inside with her virtue intact . . . and Michael on the wrong side of the door.

Her heart was pounding. He must hear it. Had he changed his mind? A moment ago, he had been holding her as if he would never let her go, but what if——

She was scared. It was as if the depth of her own need intensified her fear. What was she afraid of? It didn't matter. Only one thing mattered, being back in his arms, letting his touch send the world spinning again.

She whispered, 'Do you want to come in?'

'More than anything. Maggie.' His voice was hoarse with emotion. She saw his hand tremble as he reached for the lock, and somehow his nervousness made it easier for her.

'You forgot to lock it,' he said, pulling the key away and turning the knob to let the door sweep open.

'No.' She shook her head, panic growing as she saw the door moving. 'I never forget that. With Dixie and I living alone together, I never forget to lock it. I used to, but——' Not since the time she'd come home and found Dick firmly ensconced in the living-room.

Dick had stood to greet her, smiling, saying softly, 'Hello, Maggie, I'm back. Come to reclaim my wife.'

'Well,' said Michael now, breaking the spell of memory with his touch on her hand. 'Come on in. We'll investigate together.' He was smiling. He didn't believe she had locked the door.

She came behind him slowly, letting him pull her along, knowing someone was inside, yet knowing it couldn't be Dixie. Dixie might have had an argument with Carol and decided to come home, but if so she would have locked the door when dark came. Dick, she thought with a sick certainty.

Michael moved ahead of her towards the light in the living-room, and Maggie reviewed the evidence, her feet slow and stumbling. First there had been the letter telling her he wanted her back, and now there would be this—Dick in her home, waiting for her to come home. How had he got in? Angus had a key, but surely he wouldn't let Dick in?

Michael was still holding Maggie's hand. His fingers suddenly gripped hers painfully as his back stiffened and he demanded, 'What the hell are you doing here?'

It wasn't Dick. Maggie let out a long breath, then

stepped forward to stand beside Michael so she could see who had come into her home while she was away. The strange woman come to her feet, tall and slender in the light from the single lamp that was burning. Her eyes were on Michael, and Maggie knew her at once. While Michael had been kissing her outside, this woman had been inside, her eyes filled with the pain of betrayal.

Maggie jerked at her hand, but Michael's tightened and he said tensely, 'Maggie, I——'

'Maggie!' echoed the woman, her voice was tight and accusing. 'Is this the woman, Michael? Yes, of course it is! This is where you got the cut lip, isn't it? You wouldn't say what it was, but I knew! Maggie! Oh, yes, Heather told me about Maggie! This is the woman you've been two-timing me for, isn't it, Michael?'

'Sam, for heaven's sake!' Michael spread his hands uncomfortably and Maggie pulled her hand free of his. 'Why the hell are you here?' He turned towards Maggie and she stepped back from him with a jerk. 'Maggie——' he began, but Sam's high-pitched voice cut across his words.

'I knew something was up! I knew it wasn't just your father up here! I came to take you back, Michael.'

Maggie closed her eyes tightly, trying to shut it all out. This woman, her eyes filled with a furious pain. And Michael, looking as guilty as a man could look. This was a bad movie, but she was in the middle of it and it was all too real. She stepped back quickly as Michael turned to her. She felt a desperate urge to escape this emotional eruption. It was too much like Dick, but not even Dick had thrown her into a screaming match with another woman.

'Not me,' she said tightly, her face frozen with panic. 'Don't get me into this.'

It was like all the nightmares in the days before she

had left Dick. He didn't even look like the Michael who had held her in his arms earlier. His eyes were cold and almost hard. Maggie pulled some kind of strength around her and stared at the tall woman who was so immaculately groomed, so perfect despite her hurt anger. Angus had told her about Samantha, and Michael had not really denied that he was still involved with her. He had said something, but it must have amounted to an evasion.

'Maggie,' he was saying, and she recognised the voice that he must use in the boardroom. 'Take it easy, Maggie.' She didn't know why he was talking to her, because it was Sam who had the anger in her face. Maggie knew that hers was frozen. She herself was frozen through and through. 'Let me explain——'

'Explain?' spat out the tall, immaculate Sam. Her mouth was twisted into something hard and ugly. 'Don't bother with explain! I can explain, Maggie whoever-you-are. You're on private property, so you can damned well get off and leave——'

'Leave?' said Maggie sharply, cutting across the high tirade from Sam. She had a surging, desperate need to be alone before everything she was feeling spilled out in a dangerous eruption. She had a horrible fear that she might start crying in a minute, and she absolutely must not do that! 'If anyone is going to leave, it's going to be you!' She swung around to include Michael in her furious declaration, shouting at Sam, 'You came for him, so take him!' She congratulated herself for making her voice sound so hard and uncaring. 'If he's yours, take him and get out of here! Play out your scenes somewhere else!'

'Maggie!' Michael roared. 'I'm not some kind of toy, for passing around like——'

Maggie rushed desperately towards the door. Her

voice was rising and she didn't even try to keep it under control. She threw the door open with a crash and turned back on Michael. 'There's the door! Get out! You say he's yours, Sam whatever-*your*-name-is—take him and get out of here! And keep him! You're welcome to him! I don't need this!'

Sam was staring, maybe getting ready to make a retort. Maggie shuddered, knowing she'd totally lost her cool, but unable to recover, to stop herself from screaming, 'Get out of here! Both of you!'

'Come on, Michael!' Sam was moving towards the door, giving Michael a look that he didn't seem to see. He was staring at Maggie, angrily shaking off Sam's touch as she reached for his arm. 'I think we should go, Michael,' Sam repeated icily, eyeing Maggie as if she were a dangerous animal.

'Yes,' agreed Maggie tightly. 'You're right. You'd better go, because I can guarantee you I'm a rougher fighter than you are.' What on earth was she saying? She hadn't been in a physical fight since her tomboy battles with the neighbourhood tough boys in her early teens, but right now she would love to yank this woman's hair out of its flawless order.

Oh, God! If they would only both get out of here and leave her alone, let her close the darkness around her and get herself together.

He stopped in front of her, but she refused to meet his eyes. 'Maggie, we've got to talk. You're jumping to conclusions.'

'Conclusions?' she squeaked. 'You told me—— Damn it, Michael! Get out of here!'

Sam stopped at the door, staring at them, obviously determined not to go outside until she had Michael with her.

Maggie shouted at Michael, 'Do you think you can get

away with this? Playing around behind your girlfriend's back, trying to tell me that I'm jumping to conclusions! I had it right last week!' She was angry enough that she could meet his eyes, glaring at him hotly, screaming, 'Only I should have bitten you harder while I was at it.'

There was a second when his eyes seemed to penetrate hers, trying to see past the anger, then she was pushing him, screaming again, 'Get out!, until she had the heavy wooden barrier slammed and locked, and herself trembling on the inside, alone.

She was a fool! A crazy idiot! How could she have let this happen? Not that anything had really happened. By tomorrow she might be able to forget it, but right now she felt torn and vulnerable inside, a traitorous part of her still crying out for Michael's touch on her body. Hadn't she read somewhere that a woman's passion was stirred by her own emotional responses, not by purely physical attraction to a man? If so, she should be cold as death now, because she wanted nothing from him. Not ever. Not again.

Maggie blinked, refusing to let tears come for a man who had been touching her and watching her glow for him, intending all the time to go back to his other woman. He had played with her and it had meant nothing. She ran back to the door that she had slammed only moments ago, snapped both the lock and the dead bolt, shutting him out.

She wanted to go outside, to walk and walk until she was empty of any emotion except exhaustion, but Michael and Sam might be somewhere out there. She picked up a book and tried to read, but the characters were cardboard and dull, and sitting still was impossible. She kept seeing Michael with that woman, touching her, telling her that Maggie Simpson was nothing to him.

She gave up on the book, went to her small desk and

got out writing paper. She would catch up on her correspondence. Writing letters was a good way to remind herself of what was important in her life. Certainly none of the letters would be to Michael. She started writing her address on the paper, but the pen went dry in the middle of the second word.

There should have been half a dozen pens scattered through the drawer, but she rummaged and couldn't find even one. She decided to forget it. She had no idea who she was writing to in any case. She could write to her parents, but she had no idea what she would say. Certainly not that she had almost gone to bed with a man for the first time since she left Dick!

As if the thought of Dick had guided her fingers, she found her hand grasping the folded pages of his last letter to her. She should have thrown it out. If Dixie found it and read it she would start campaigning for her parents to reunite, for Maggie to write to Dick and open her arms. She closed her eyes painfully. She didn't need to open the folds of paper to see the words again. He had written the same lies she had heard so many times before.

After those years with Dick, how could she be fool enough to let another man tell her lies? 'What about your woman?' she had asked. He'd shrugged it off, saying, 'We're not in love with each other.' A lie, because a woman would not follow her man and make a scene like that if she did not care about him.

Dancing in his arms, it had not even occurred to her that he might be lying. She had almost taken him into her bed. Well, going to bed with a man wasn't any big deal these days, was it? It had not happened, would not happen.

Her breasts were still swollen, as if waiting for his touch. She took a deep breath and tried to make the

wanting pass. Michael MacAvoy would have to find his
pleasures somewhere else in future.

She was going to bed, to sleep. He wasn't going to
keep her awake all night, thinking and remembering and
needing things she did not want. She went into the bedroom and changed into a thin nightgown, then unfolded
the sofa bed and lay in it, eyes closed and willing sleep.

Of course it was no good. Damn! Why did she have to
be such an agoniser? Why couldn't she shake this off and
be practical, forget Michael and Dick, and just live her
life as she chose? She got up and moved through the
dark into her small kitchen. She hated hot milk, so she
added chocolate and honey. It tasted sweet and soothing.
She turned out the light and drank it in the dark,
picturing Michael making love to Sam.

The air inside was close, suffocating. She opened the
door to the small veranda at the back of her little house,
and stood there, feeling the cool night air through her
thin gown.

Then she heard Michael's footsteps. It had to be
Michael. She would swear she recognised his step. He
was alone and he couldn't see her. There was no way on
earth he could know she was standing outside on the
patio. She was on the far side of the little house from
him, out of sight. She shivered, terrified that he would
step aboard, walk around the edge of her barge and find
her here.

She hugged herself tightly when he knocked, feeling
her own flesh through the thin gown. He must not come
around, must not see her.

'Maggie!'

He sounded impatient. Funny, when she'd met him
she had thought him the most controlled man she knew.
She trembled, knowing she had to get the door closed
somehow. If she stayed here in the open, she would give

herself away by some sound, and he would be standing in front of her, seeing far too much. Shivering, she stepped back inside the door, trying not to rustle, to make any sound for him. His voice carried clearly to her, calling out her name again, but she wouldn't let herself hear. She carefully slid the back door closed. The latch made a noise as she locked it. She moved into the living-room and sat down on the edge of the sofa as if poised for flight.

'Maggie, I know you're there! I want to talk to you!'

She huddled, shivering, and it seemed a long time before she became aware of her own thoughts. Panicking, shivering inside as if she were terrified. She closed her eyes, remembered another night. Dick outside, calling her name, pounding on the door until she finally let him in. Once more in a merry-go-round cycle.

'Go away, Mickey. Please go away!' It was anger at being put through this same crazy, helpless nightmare again that enabled her to make her voice strong and hard.

She stood up, staring at the door, listening to the silence for a long time. She knew he had not gone away, even before he spoke. His voice sounded very quiet, very rational.

'Maggie, let me in. We have to talk to each other.'

She shook her head, silently, but she could have sworn that he saw, because he said gently through the door, 'Open the door, sweetheart. Please. I just want to see that you're all right, then I'll go. We can talk tomorrow.'

'No.' She shivered. He had no right to call her sweetheart when it didn't mean anything.

Where was her house-coat? It was so cold in here now. She moved quietly, found her house-coat hanging on the back of her bathroom door. She belted it around her, listening for Michael's breathing on the other side of the door. She had no idea why he was so determined to see her, but she knew what he was doing. He was working out his strategy, figuring out how to get her to open the door. Sooner or later he would find a way.

She walked to the door, slowly slid the bolt back and took the spring lock off. Then she opened the door and stood still, staring out at him. She had not turned on any lights, so it was unlikely that he could see anything in her face.

'I'm fine,' she said tonelessly. She had to talk very carefully to keep the emotion from showing through. She wasn't sure what all the emotions were. There was anger, but there was more, and he must not see.

He was staring at her, but she could not read the expression in his eyes in the half-light. Around his mouth the lines looked deep and strained. He reached out as if to touch her, but she tensed and shook her head. His hand went to his own hair, raking through and sending his curls wild and unruly.

'You look tired,' she said, surprising herself, but he looked strangely vulnerable for Michael.

He smiled ruefully. 'It's been quite an evening, Maggie. Can I come in? Please.'

He knew that she was going to say no before her head moved. He felt like a heel all over again, because the strain on her face was his fault. He had never thought of himself as an unfaithful man, but he had certainly done his best to seduce Maggie while Sam was still living under his roof in Victoria.

Her voice was only a whisper now. 'Go away, Mickey. Please go away!' It was the look on her face that defeated him, the crazy mixture of anger and fear. He didn't understand it, but he couldn't fight it.

'Tomorrow,' he said raggedly, pushing his hands into his pockets. What was she afraid of? 'Tomorrow, Maggie, we have to talk.' She didn't respond with words, but he thought that she nodded before the door closed again between them.

He couldn't sleep, so he went walking on the shore. Heaven knew what time it was. It felt as if the night were lasting for ever.

A siren wailed, then a police car went tearing past in pursuit of some invisible quarry. The moon was gone, leaving an inky-black sky overhead. He couldn't even see a star. He remembered the way Maggie had stirred in his arms, as if her soft, heated body were making promises to his.

A taxi passed him, slowing down. He didn't raise his hand. He needed to be alone to think, to decide what he was going to do next. Sam was at a hotel uptown but, although they hadn't settled everything tonight, the explosion that would end their relationship was well under way.

He felt thoroughly ashamed of his behaviour towards Sam, but it was not Sam that worried him now. He had to straighten things out with Maggie. Somehow. Then—he didn't know what came next, but for Maggie he had to keep a clear, cool head. He concentrated on that, walking alone through the streets.

Somehow he must talk to her, make her understand . . .

Understand that he was living with one woman, pursuing another? How the hell was he going to get her to see that in a favourable light?

It had been a mistake, trying to talk to her tonight. He had to give her time to calm down. Maggie needed careful handling. He remembered with a shock that he had not come north to wage the battle of men and women with Maggie. He had come to look after his father.

Despite his own unexpected attraction to Maggie, he still had to settle his father's problems, and that was one more reason why he had to talk to Maggie.

CHAPTER SIX

JAN knocked on Maggie's door at dawn the next morning, calling out, 'Maggie! Hey, wake up! We're sailing! Want to come?'

It was like a heaven-sent escape. Later, Michael would be at her door, wanting to talk. Did he want to apologise? Or suggest that they carry on an affair behind Sam's back? Either way, Maggie did not want to listen. She stumbled out of bed and opened the door to Jan, glancing over to make sure there was no sign of movement yet on Angus's boat.

'Put on the coffee-pot, Jan,' she told her friend. 'I'll just get dressed and then phone Dixie to get down here from Carol's.'

She was nervous that Michael would appear before she could get away, relieved when she and Dixie were on board and sailing away before there was any sign of life from *Sasha*. Heaven knew what she thought Michael would do! In the broad light of day, he would probably decide he had been insane the night before. He would avoid her eyes and head back to Victoria as soon as he could.

All day, sailing out in Chatham Sound, Maggie concentrated on thinking of things that had nothing to do with Michael. By the time she and Dixie returned home from their sailing trip that night, Michael was gone and she was able to tell herself that she really was glad she had escaped him.

She wished Dixie would stop mentioning Michael's name, but her daughter seemed entranced with Angus's son. All through the next week Maggie tried to ignore it, but Dixie was hard to ignore.

'Did Mickey kiss you when you went out dancing?' she asked casually one evening.

'Dixie, that's none of your business!' Maggie wished she had kept her voice casual, because Angus was across the table and his eyes looked suddenly alert and curious.

Dixie took a deep breath and said quickly, 'If you're not going to marry my dad again, you could marry Mickey instead.'

Maggie pushed her chair back with a crash, her cheeks flaming with anger. 'Dixie, if you want a father, you—I guess that's a problem you'll have to work out on your own.'

Through the rest of the week Dixie didn't mention Michael. Maggie spent a lot of time deliberately trying to picture him with Sam. Reality therapy, she told herself, but it was unexpectedly painful.

On Friday Angus suddenly said, 'Maggie, it's going to be a cold winter.' And then he started to tell her how he had come to own his boat.

His wife, whose name had also been Sasha, had always been an impulsive woman with a weakness for lotteries. When she was lucky enough to win a major prize, she had bought the boat for her and Angus to retire on. They had named it *Windfall.* Then, when Sasha had tragically died just before Angus had planned to retire, he renamed the vessel and left Victoria, turning the business over to Michael and going where he felt closest to the memory of his wife.

Maggie wanted to cry, but Angus was standing stiffly on the wharf, avoiding looking at her. They were both silent for a long time, then Angus said, 'Michael will be here this weekend.'

Maggie said quickly, 'Dixie and I are going to Prince

George to visit my Mom and Dad.' He said nothing, but she felt ashamed, as if she were running from something she should be able to face up to.

She had to avoid Michael until she got over this physical attraction. Even though driving to Prince George on a two-day weekend was insane, she was determined to go. It was a thousand-mile round trip and she couldn't afford the petrol, but she would put the fuel on her credit card. Sooner or later it would have to be paid, but this weekend it was easier to face another overdraft than to face Michael.

She picked up Dixie after school on Friday and tried to smile as if it were a fun trip. That lasted until Dixie started wailing, 'Can't we visit Grandpa and Grandma some other time?'

'Definitely not!' she said, picturing Michael walking along the floats, looking for her. She remembered coming home with his arm around her last week, and Sam waiting for them. It occurred to her that Michael had seemed more concerned about Maggie's reaction that night than Sam's, but she pushed the thought away.

Useless to pretend that she should battle him over Angus. If Michael did succeed in taking Angus south with him, Maggie and Dixie would miss their neighbour, but Angus wouldn't suffer. He was already dreading the cold of winter in the north, and she had seen the pleasure in his eyes when he looked at Michael. He missed his son.

Dixie's sulking filled the car. 'Mom——'

'Dixie, we're driving to Prince George!'

At the top of Rainbow Mountain, Dixie was volubly hungry. By the time they came down the mountain to drive along the river, she was thirsty. Maggie was angry. She stopped the car.

'Are we turning around?' asked Dixie hopefully.

'No! There's a creek over on the other side of the road. Go get yourself a drink!' Maggie gripped the wheel and stared at the empty highway ahead.

'With what?' asked the sullen Dixie.

Maggie said sharply, 'Do it like a caveman. Bend down and scoop up the water with your hands!'

Dixie stormed out of the car and across the highway. An eighteen-wheeler rig roared past and Maggie shuddered, terrified by a vision of an angry Dixie being hit by the massive truck.

She couldn't bring herself to apologise for her anger, but in Terrace she pulled into McDonalds and got them both a Big Mac and a large Coke. Then she had to stop at the Royal Bank banking machine to replenish her cash. Darn! She would be overdrawn again before the week was over.

What if Michael used her absence to spirit Angus away from them? What if she and Dixie came back on Sunday night and found themselves alone? She blinked away tears and concentrated on the yellow line that ran down the middle of the highway. She would miss Angus terribly. This was insanity! Crossing half the province to avoid a man, then spending the weekend wishing she were with him.

Normally, Maggie would have enjoyed the brief visit to her parents, but this weekend was a disaster from the beginning. By the time Maggie started driving back on Sunday, she felt drained and depressed.

The drive back was long and exhausting. Dixie was silent throughout, sulking over an argument she had had with her grandfather. When they finally drove down the hill into Prince Rupert, Maggie was glad to hear Dixie ask in a normal voice, 'Can we go swimming before we go home? We've got our suits with us, and it's public swim time.'

Maggie had packed their bathing-suits to use in the swimming pool at her parents' apartment building. She had no energy for swimming herself, but she would love to climb into the whirlpool and relax for half an hour before they went home. She pulled the car up at the civic centre complex without argument.

Dixie ran ahead into the aquatic centre, waving her season pass at the cashier and leaving her mother to pay her own way in. The cashier greeted Maggie with a cheerful, 'Hi, Maggie!' although Maggie hadn't a clue who the woman was.

Dixie must have shot out of her clothes and into her bathing-suit in record time. There was no sign of her in the changing-rooms—just the arm of her sweatshirt hanging out of an unlocked locker. Maggie added her own clothes and put a quarter in the slot. She pinned the locker key on to the shoulder of her black bathing-suit.

She left her contact lenses on. Last year she'd lost a lens in the water, but she wasn't swimming today, just taking a lazy soak in the whirlpool and trying to get rid of the shaky exhaustion from driving a thousand miles in a couple of days.

She sank down into the hot green water of the whirlpool, letting the heat seep through her bones. Running from Michael. That was a laugh! By this time he had probably stopped pursuing her. Most men gave up the pursuit after a while. Even Dick's overtures seemed to have dropped off in frequency to once a year or so.

She opened her eyes, deciding that her real problem was her dispostion. It seemed that she had been cranky towards Dixie all weekend. There was a bearded man sitting across from her, watching her. She met his stare without smiling. After a moment he looked away. Beside him was a woman with a young son. The chubby boy kept getting away from his mother, splashing into the hot water. Once he fell across Maggie's legs and she set him on his feet again.

The L-shaped swimming pool beside the whirlpool was a sea of moving faces and bodies. Maybe she needed a new eye prescription, because she couldn't seem to see very well. She thought she saw Dixie once, flinging a beach ball into the air. She even imagined she saw Michael in the swarming sea of bodies, and that proved she needed new lenses.

Standing up made her dizzy. Too much heat, or was it a lack of food? She had hardly eaten all weekend. She went over to the showers and turned on the cold water. Then, shivering, she went into the sauna and stood looking out through the glass wall.

Dixie was playing water polo with three other youngsters and two men. Maggie watched her daughter in her bright blue bathing-suit, flying at the taller man in an enthusiastic tackle, fighting for possession of the ball. The man flung the ball away. Dixie abandoned her tackle, swimming after the ball. Laughing, the man pushed back a wet lock of hair from his forehead, muscles rippling across his bare shoulders. Then he chased after Dixie, catching her just as she took aim and fired towards the basket.

The ball missed. Dixie tore off after it, wading and splashing through a sea of bodies. It was hard to tell at this distance, but Maggie thought he was smiling as he watched her daughter. It was Michael. She had known that it was him. She had been weak and trembling at the knees from the moment she'd spotted him from the whirlpool.

When the ball came his way again, he leapt for it, then he was buried in a blanket of enthusiastic young bodies. With all those arms and legs flying, it was a wonder he didn't get hurt, but he was up again, throwing the ball to Dixie's eager arms. He looked as if he were having the time of his life.

Once he turned and looked straight towards her. Could he see her through the darkened glass of the sauna? She stepped back just as two teenage boys came in, dodging around her on their way to the wooden seats. She walked away from the window and went into the darkest corner of the sauna, lying down on the highest bench and closing her eyes.

After a while her heartbeat slowed and she got her breathing under control. She tensed when she heard the door open, but it was only the boys leaving.

Why was Michael at the pool? He couldn't possibly have expected to find her here, or Dixie. She was achingly glad to see him, and terrified—both at the same time.

She should get up and go, wait for Dixie in the changing-room. No, damn it! She wasn't going to keep running like a coward! It was just sex appeal, or something to do with hormones and her thirtieth birthday coming next year. Whatever the cause, she could not spend her life running from the man.

If Michael was still here, it meant Angus had not gone either. If it wasn't too late, maybe she could find a way to convince Michael that his father was better left here in the north. In a minute she would stand up and go out there. She would give him a bright smile, as if he were a friend she were pleased to see, but not as if the sight of him filled her with a painful joy.

The door opened. She kept her eyes closed, breathed slowly and deeply, listening to silent footsteps, and she knew who it was before he sat beside her. She was lying on her back. When she opened her eyes, his face was only inches from hers.

'Hello, sweetheart.' His voice flowed along her veins, a delicious resonance within her. He seemed very large, and very naked, sitting there with drops of water glistening on his arms, wearing only a brief pair of red trunks. His eyes moved down along her feminine form, taking in the white skin exposed by the deep V of her neckline, the curve of her abdomen through the black bathing-suit, the milky white of her thighs. His voice was gruff. 'You've been avoiding me, Maggie.'

She licked her lips, saw his eyes follow the movement. 'Shouldn't you be in Victoria?' Her voice should have had more strength. She tried again. 'You can't get another plane until tomorrow. You've got a business to run, haven't you? Angus said you're all wrapped up in your business—night and day. Weekends.'

'I'm bewitched,' he said softly. 'I had to see you, Maggie.' His eyes couldn't seem to leave the quick rising and falling of her breasts.

She said desperately, 'I don't—— You——' She took a deep breath, finally said bluntly, ' What about Sam?'

He nodded and said sombrely, 'I know, Maggie. I didn't—I don't feel very good about that.' He lifted her hand, turned it so that he could stare at the lines of her palm. 'I don't really know what to say to you about Sam. Except——' He shrugged, his fingers tightening in a brief spasm on her wrist. 'It's over. Sam moved out last week.'

Maggie stared at his bronzed fingers against her white skin. 'You're very tanned. Did you get that in Victoria?'

'Hawaii,' he said briefly. 'Maggie——'

'So you do take holidays? Angus said you were all business, but I guess that's not always true.' Michael shifted impatiently and she said abruptly, 'You said you and Sam weren't in love with each other.'

'Maggie, I didn't—— Oh, damn, Maggie! There's no

way I can come out of this one without looking like a heel. I—I just want you to know that it's not my usual style.' He smiled a little, then his face grew still and intent as he traced the curve of her cheek with a gentle fingertip. 'I'm really not capable of handling more than one woman at a time,' he said softly.

She struggled to sit up. He was too close, leaning over her. She had to stop her hands clinging to him for support. He bent, his lips brushing hers in a soft, erotic caress. 'Maggie, I'll die if I can't kiss you soon.'

She pulled back, but there was nowhere to go. He shifted and put an arm on either side of her, supporting himself and imprisoning her at once. She said desperately, 'I'll bite you again!' His lips were moving closer. His bare chest was covered with short, curling hair. The muscles stood out on his broad shoulders as he bent down.

'I'll take a chance,' he said, covering her lips with the gentlest of kisses. The hairs of his chest brushed teasingly against the damp skin above her bathing-suit. With every ragged breath she took, she could feel her chest touching his.

His arms were surrounding her, so close. She could feel his breath on her skin, could smell an erotic mixture of Michael's natural scent and the cedar planks of the sauna. She was propped up on her elbows, hands flattened on the cedar. She tried to tell herself she was trapped, but she knew that if her hands were free they would be reaching up to touch the curling hair on his chest.

'Why do you spend so much time running from me, Maggie?'

She shifted to free one arm, pushed her hand through her curls. They fell damply back on to her forehead. She tossed them back, spraying Michael with a fine shower of water.

'I went to visit my parents,' she said, although it was no answer at all. His fingers lifted to trace a curl that lay against her cheek.

He said, 'I almost followed you,' and she believed him. All weekend she had been paralysed by the sound of the doorbell, expecting Michael's voice each time her mother had opened the door. Her father had noticed her watching the door.

Now Michael's fingers traced the curve of her cheek, the sharp angle of her cheekbone. 'Maggie, you've been hiding from me ever since that scene with Sam.'

Sooner or later someone would come into this darkened sauna. When they did, Michael would have to take his hand away from her neck. She trembled as his fingers traced lightly down from her throat, brushing the swelling above her bathing-suit. She pushed his hand away, but it made no difference. He was so close that she could feel his heat without touching. His hand turned and entrapped hers, his fingers caressing her wrist again. She had never realised what trembling, sensuous nerves were buried under the flesh of her inner wrist.

'I have been avoiding you,' she admitted. How could she tell him her reasons? It was not only Sam, but more her own fears. Even now she felt uncomfortable about the pleasure she felt in his nearness.

'Maggie, it's over with Sam.' He cupped her chin, tipping her face up until her eyes met his again. 'I was unforgivably slow about telling her, but it was over after the first time I kissed you—the time you bit me, damn you! I—Maggie, I don't want to talk about Sam. I want to talk about us.'

His lips were closer, and she knew hers would soon open to welcome his kiss. She said breathlessly, desperately, 'It wasn't just her. I've been avoiding you because I—because this scares me. I haven't been involved with anyone for a long time. Not like this. I don't really want to——'

'We'll take it very slowly,' he said softly. His lips took hers in a deep kiss that seemed to go on for ever.

She gasped, 'You've got to be joking! You're not exactly taking your time!' She managed to struggle to a sitting position.

Another couple came into the sauna and he had to stop kissing her. He leaned back against the wall with one arm draped casually across her legs.

'Dixie's a tiger at water polo,' he told her, his eyes on the beginning of the hollow between her breasts. 'She's a nice kid.'

'She wasn't nice this weekend.' She watched her fingertips tracing the damp hairs on his arm. She told herself that she should stop touching him, stop drawing pleasure from his dark virility, but her fingers did not listen. 'Dixie didn't want to go to Prince George, and she wouldn't let me forget it all weekend.'

'How were your parents?' The grey of his eyes deepened. Under her touch, his arm had tensed in a spasmodic response.

'Fine,' she said, smiling a little, trembling because she could read his mind, and he wasn't thinking about her parents. 'My dad raked me over the coals about Dixie because they got into a big fight.'

Michael's hand curved around her calf. She tried to stop the trembling that crawled up her leg, but she couldn't. He said softly, 'What a couple of hotheads you two are!'

The look in his eyes made her tongue stumble. 'Dad—er—suggested we both move back home. Dixie cried, and I shouted. My mother intervened and somehow managed to change the subject.'

He said, 'I have a suggestion——' but she broke in quickly, overriding his words, 'We're doing just fine, Dixie and I. I've got a job I like, and a home. But Dad will never accept that I can look after myself.' She was terrified that he would go on, suggesting something like the arrangement he had had with Sam, whatever that was. Thankfully, he was easily distracted. He stood up and held his hand out to her.

Outside the sauna, the lifeguard called 'time'. Michael said, 'Shall we go, Maggie?'

She let him imprison her hand as they went out to the pool deck. She was very conscious of his muscular legs and chest beside her, of the way his brief red swimming-trunks clung to his body.

Dixie bounced out of the water and came dashing towards them with the ball imprisoned under her arm. The lifeguard shouted and Dixie's steps slowed almost to a walk.

'I won!' she announced to them both.

'Of course you did,' said Michael, dropping an arm around each of them and turning towards the changing-rooms. 'Why don't you ladies change and we'll pick up an ice-cream on the way home?'

'All *right*!' said Dixie, dodging away towards the ladies' changing-room, calling back, 'Hurry up, Mom! I'm starving!'

'I wish she'd settle down a bit,' said Maggie ruefully.

Michael squeezed her shoulder. 'She's all right. She's enjoying life, and the world can take a little noise from children. You wouldn't want her like my nieces, would you?'

'A little,' Maggie admitted, then shook her head. 'I'm sure they're well behaved in company, and they pick up after themselves, but——'

'Yes, but—— ' he agreed feelingly.

When they had finished changing, Michael was waiting for them outside the changing-room. He took her arm and Dixie's hand, announcing, 'We'll go in your car, Maggie.'

She didn't want to feel this warm weakness at the tone of his voice. He sounded as if it were natural, their going together. As if they were a couple. As if he had traded Sam in on Maggie. She forced that thought to the front of her mind, because it seemed to help her think clearly.

If she had been alone, she would have been tempted to leave the car and walk home. She was too tired for driving, and perhaps that was why she let him take the keys from her hand.

'It's not a major concession,' he said softly. 'If I drive your car, it doesn't mean you've lost the battle.'

'The battle?' She pulled her jacket tightly around herself. 'Are we fighting a battle?' They had been fighting for Angus, but this was a different battle, one that she couldn't afford to be involved in.

He didn't answer, but he arranged the seating the way he wanted, with Dixie in the back, and Maggie beside him where he could move his hand to cover hers. She kept feeling that she should pull away from his touch, but it seemed silly, shying away from pleasures. What on earth was there to be afraid of?

Who would care if she had a brief affair with Michael MacAvoy? Evidently not Dixie, because Maggie's daughter jumped out of the car at Rushbrooke, gave their linked hands an approving glance, then swung the shoulder-bag that held their weekend supplies over her shoulder and started off towards the floats.

Michael squeezed her hand as she hurried to follow Dixie. 'I want to be alone with you.' She glanced at the boats and the people and he added, 'I know this isn't exactly privacy, but we're relatively alone. We can talk.'

'You're dreaming!' He didn't understand what she meant, but they had gone only two boat lengths when she became involved in a conversation with a thin, elderly man who was trying to decide whether to use epoxy or copper bottom-paint.

'Are you an expert on bottom-paint?' asked Michael when he succeeded in drawing her away.

She smiled, looking back at the grey-haired man who walked too fast for his age. 'He didn't want an expert. He just wanted to talk about it.'

Michael slipped her arm through his, holding her closer as they walked. 'Do you look after them all? My father? And this elderly fellow? Solly and Rex with their dog wars? Anybody who asks?'

She said defensively, 'Why not? It's a better life than sitting in front of a typewriter. My typing's rotten, anyway.'

He was silent as they walked back to her home, and she had no idea what he was thinking. She avoided looking at his face. The feel of his arm under her hand was upsetting enough to her equilibrium.

Inside her home she found Angus with a beer in his hand, already deep in a game of draughts with Dixie. Michael seemed very quiet, but alert, as if he were working out some strategy. He accepted a beer from Maggie and sat down to watch the game.

'Hear about the Alaskan earthquake?' asked Angus.

Maggie asked, 'When? How big a quake?'

'Not a big one.' Angus picked up his draughts piece and jumped over two of Dixie's. Dixie groaned and Angus said, 'I heard it on the radio. No injuries, not much property damage.'

Maggie's eyes darkened. 'Angus, there wasn't any word of a tsunami warning?'

'No, Maggie. No tidal wave.' He grinned as Dixie

retaliated by jumping three of his men, making Maggie wonder if Angus was deliberately letting her daughter win.

Maggie didn't know exactly what Michael was up to. He kept watching her, and Angus seemed to be watching them both and smiling a lot. If Angus thought this was a romance, like his with Sasha, then he was in for a disappointment. At the most, it might develop into a brief, hot affair. Maggie was unsure whether Angus would understand that.

Angus seemed determined to encourage any sign of romance between his son and his neighbour. He started yawning just as Maggie was sending Dixie off to bed.

Michael said, 'I'll walk over with you, Dad. I want to get my jacket.' His eyes found Maggie's as he added, 'Then I'll come back and take Maggie out for a walk.'

Maggie had no chance to say anything before they were gone. To Dixie, she said, 'School tomorrow. Bedtime now.' Dixie frowned and Maggie said, 'I'm a terrible spoilsport, aren't I, honey?'

'You're not kidding,' grumbled Dixie, but she disappeared into the bedroom they shared, tossing back, 'Mom, if you and Mickey want to go out, I'll be OK. Grandpa Angus is right next door.'

Maggie managed to keep her tongue, determined that she would not get pulled into that kind of conversation with Dixie. She had not forgotten Dixie's suggestion that she marry to supply a father for her daughter.

Michael was gone for about fifteen minutes, then he came back, letting himself in without knocking. Seeing him standing there, she felt a strong urge to stand up and go to him, to run her fingers through his hair. After swimming, his curls were springing free, making him look very unlike a corporate takeover man.

He crossed the room very slowly, his eyes never

leaving her. She felt the colour come up in her cheeks and knew he saw it. She wanted him to touch her, kiss her, but Dixie was probably listening carefully to every sound.

'What's wrong, Maggie?' He was very close now, and she could see that he had shaved while he was gone with Angus.

In her mind she tried out the words, 'Dixie's listening to us,' but she felt ridiculously embarrassed to say them. It would be like saying, 'I know you're going to kiss me.'

He reached down and removed the book from her hands. He glanced at the title, then said, 'You don't want to read that now, do you?'

She shook her head mutely. She wanted him to kiss her, but she was going to have to send him away. He dropped the book on to the coffee-table.

'Come here, Maggie,' he urged, low-voiced. He caught her hand and pulled her to her feet.

'Mickey!' she muttered, using his childhood nickname as if it were a weapon. He shook his head, grinning. He led her across the room, picked up her coat and opened the door. 'I'm not going out,' she whispered. 'I don't want to——'

'Liar,' he accused softly, catching her and the coat together in his arms, pressing his lips down on to hers. She breathed in the scent of him, a spicy aftershave blended with his own musky maleness. 'You're afraid,' he accused, taunting softly.

'It's late,' she whispered, suddenly panic-stricken, 'and Dixie——'

'Take a chance,' he urged softly, his hands holding her shoulders, his thumbs kneading gently.

She closed her eyes briefly. Take a chance. Impetuous though she was by nature, she had learned to be careful, to keep herself in check where there was danger. Was this danger? Michael, his hands on her, his eyes telling her she was a beautiful, desirable woman. If she went out of the door with him, she would be opening herself to an intimacy she had avoided for years. Well, why not? She was twenty-nine. She had been married, for heaven's sake! She knew how to look after herself.

'Stop thinking so much.' Michael's voice was low in her ear, 'Dad is close by if Dixie needs anything.'

She slipped out of his arms, on to the float. When she looked around the darknened waterfront, she could see silhouettes of boats, black water melding with even blacker mountains. The beauty of it surged through her like a pain. Behind her, Michael touched her waist.

CHAPTER SEVEN

MICHAEL opened the door of the hotel room with a key, holding it for her. She stepped past him, avoiding his eyes. She walked towards the window, taking in the comfortable easy chair, the soft elegance of expensive upholstery and oak furnishings, the large mirror reflecting a deep red brocade bedspread covering the double bed.

She slid open the glass door and stepped out on to the balcony to escape him for a moment. Michael's footsteps were muted, almost soundless on the thick carpet behind her. She glanced back when she heard soft, romantic music playing. Michael was just moving away from a portable stereo tape deck.

She turned back quickly, looking out over the darkened harbour. It was all prepared in advance, as if she were a pawn in a game he was playing. He hadn't stopped at the desk to register, just slipped her hand through his arm and guided her to the elevator—in silence, because she'd been frozen, and he had felt her tension.

Maggie had been successfully manipulated into the lion's den. She felt nervous and angry. She wished she had refused to come. She tensed as she heard his footsteps behind her. He touched her shoulder lightly, set two glasses filled with pale liquid on the rail of the balcony. She tried to tune him out, to pretend he wasn't there, but of course it didn't work.

She was terribly aware of her own body, conscious of his eyes watching her. When she glanced up, quickly,

116

she found him smiling as if he enjoyed looking at her. Down below, the streets were very quiet. Maggie concentrated on a solitary pedestrian walking slowly towards the downtown area.

'You had this evening all worked out,' she said tonelessly, keeping her eyes on the movement below.

He didn't answer her accusation, but he moved closer, his long fingers brushing her hair back from her cheek. The curls sprung back at once, twisting around his hand. He found the underside of her chin and exerted a light pressure, until she was facing him, looking into his eyes. She tried to turn back, to watch the anonymous man down on the street, but his fingers tightened, holding her.

Her tongue nervously moistened her lips. She knew that he was manipulating her, that she would feel stronger without his hands touching, his eyes watching so intently. He knew it too, but his expressionless facial muscles gave away none of his own feelings.

She said breathlessly, 'A walk, you said. You didn't say where. No word of our destination, and you were laughing when I hesitated.'

'Maggie——' He broke off, shook his head slightly, and for a second she thought that he looked uncertain, vulnerable.

She stepped back from his fingers, but she immediately came up against the hard corner of the balcony. If only he didn't watch her like that, as if he could see everything. 'Why did you rent a hotel room?' she demanded abruptly. She gestured towards the double bed inside the room. 'For this? You didn't ask me! You just came up here—when? Yesterday? Today?—and rented a hotel room, fitted it out with your fancy stereo and romantic music, brought in drink and——' Her voice was rising. She took a big gulp, then let the rest of the words out. 'You set up the mood and then you went out hunting for your prey. You probably even had the swimming pool thing worked out. How did you know I'd be at the pool tonight?'

The low sincerity of his voice penetrated her anger. 'Maggie, I admit that I seem to be making a mess of this, but the swimming pool wasn't planned. That was an unexpected bonus.'

'But the rest?'

She had no intention of trying to control her anger. The anger kept away the dangerous, soft vulnerability, but he said softly, 'Shhh,' and she found herself silent. He leaned closer. 'It depends on your point of view, doesn't it, sweetheart? Your *facts* are right.'

'Facts,' she repeated, watching him warily. 'What else is there but the facts? You came up here with the intention of—of seducing me.'

He touched her cheek fleetingly. 'I don't deny the hotel room, or the music. Well, the music seemed like a good idea, because I wouldn't have chosen to take you to a hotel in normal circumstances. I thought it might help give a better atmosphere.' He grinned self-consciously. 'The bed is a little prominent in the room, and—well, it lacks a bit in subtlety.'

She found herself giggling, then frowning. 'Why are you doing all this? Why didn't you go back home yesterday?'

'Tsunami,' he said softly.

'What do you mean?' She could hardly breathe. His eyes had turned almost opaque as he moved closer. If she moved her arm, she could reach out and touch his face.

'A tsunami is a tidal wave, isn't it?'

'Basically,' she agreed. 'It's a very large sea wave

produced by an underwater quake or eruption.'

He nodded. 'Rising up from underneath, sweeping over everything. That's how you hit my life, Maggie. I came up here with everything in order—like sheltered waters with only ripples on the surface. And you swept over my life like a tsunami!'

He pushed away from her, pacing the balcony with a restlessness she had never seen in him before. 'I can't stay away, darling, but whenever we start to get close, someone walks in—my father, Dixie. Yes, I do want to make love with you. I had an idea that you wanted it, too.'

He stopped talking and she had to nod, because she couldn't forget how his arms had felt. He said hoarsely, 'I wanted to be alone with you, and when we're alone, things happen. I want to touch you, and when I touch you——'He laughed unsteadily before he said, 'The world sort of explodes. It seemed a good idea to be prepared for that.'

The moon had risen, throwing the large freighters in the harbour into sharp silhouette against the sky. Maggie could not say a word. Michael said, 'Maggie, bringing you here doesn't mean we have to make love.' His fingers brushed the hair at the back of her neck, making the flesh tremble. 'We can watch the moonlight, even watch television if you like. I'd just like to be with you, alone.'

She did not know what words to use. He had all the words, and his voice was careful, as if he were judging the effect of each syllable as it left his lips. He said, 'I'll take you home if you like.'

When she turned around, slowly, he was standing very still, very close, 'It's dark,' she said unsteadily. 'I can't see what you're thinking.' She wanted very badly to move into his arms, to give herself up to the feelings welling up in her. She wasn't sure what held her back.

'That's probably just as well,' he said. He pushed both hands into his pockets, as if he had to imprison his hands to keep from touching her. He moved away, picked up his drink and raised it to his lips. She watched him swallow.

'Shall I take you home, Maggie?'

She was silent, knowing that soon he would close the distance between them, take her in his arms. It felt as if she had been waiting for his arms all her life.

'Want to watch television?' he asked, a hint of laughter behind his words. She shook her head. 'Talk, then?' he asked.

'I suppose,' she whispered. There were so many things she wanted to know about him, but she was caught in a wordless spell. She felt as if her mind were saying things to his, receiving answers without words.

He seemed to be closer, but he hadn't moved. 'Are you going to take your coat off?'

She nodded, but made no move to take it off. Why wasn't he touching her? She moved to him. He remained very still, watching her. When she was close enough, she realised that he was as nervous as she was.

'My coat,' she whispered, and his fingers moved to her buttons. Trembling fingers. She watched as the buttons emerged from their holes. The top one, then the middle. The lower one, then Michael's hands pushing the coat gently away from her shoulders.

Her eyes rose to his face. He was watching, following the motion of her coat as it slipped away from her shoulders. It fell to the deck of the balcony. His eyes moved over the curve of her breasts, paused to caress the soft skin of her throat.

'Maggie, if you want to talk, you'll have to come up with the words.' His hands moved lightly along her arms. She had trouble getting the air in and out of her lungs. Then she managed one deep breath, and she could see his awareness of the way her breasts moved under her light sweater.

'I'm always talking,' she said unsteadily, a wild joy surging through her. 'Tell me—tell me what you're working on now. Angus says you're always starting something new.'

'Products?' He saw the mischief in her eyes, managed to sound almost casual himself. 'Twelve-volt generating systems, mostly. Power's a problem anywhere away from civilisation, so—wind or solar——' He was having trouble keeping his train of thought as she stepped closer into the circle of his arms.

Her hands settled against his chest and she tipped her head back to watch him. He wasn't smiling with his lips, but his eyes were like fire. Her fingers slipped under the lapels of his jacket, and she felt her palms tingling at the wonderful warmth of him.

'There's not much sun up here in the winter,' she said slowly. His hands slipped around her, his fingers spreading out over her back. 'Lots of wind, though,' she said breathlessly. She would remember this night for ever. 'Tell me about wind generators, Michael.'

His fingers were exploring the curves beneath her sweater, just touching her outlines. His voice was husky. 'The problem is to generate power in low winds, yet . . .' His thumbs rubbed gently against the soft skin below her ribs, soothing the trembling they created.

She tried to keep her eyes open, tried to focus on his face. 'Yet?' she prompted.

'Can't overdrive the generator in high winds.' He lifted his hands to her face, holding it very gently, his fingers curved into the curls, supporting her head. His breath was coming quick and shallow. She watched his eyes change, darken almost to black as he breathed.

'I'd rather talk about you, Maggie. I want to kiss you.'

She felt his muscles ripple under her fingers. 'I wanted to hear about the generators,' she teased, letting her hands wander. He was very close, his breath fanning her face. She shuddered in anticipation. 'Oh, Michael . . . '

'If you want generators from me,' he growled, his lips descending to hers, 'then get farther away.'

His lips drank in her softness, his fingers caressing her face, her scalp, drawing her close. She opened to his probing tongue, returning his invasion of her mouth in a dizzying response that left them both trembling.

Her fingers tangled through his hair, transforming well-disciplined waves into frantic curls. She pulled him closer as his mouth moved intimately along her throat, possessing the tip of her earlobe. Then his arms came down, taking her close, drawing her body against his until her breasts crushed against his chest and his thighs pressed hard against her. She could hardly hear what he said for the ringing, singing in her ears.

'What?' she breathed.

'Permanent magnet motors.' He was trembling, so he took her closely in his arms and leaned against the doorway. He shifted a little, allowing one hand access to the round temptation of her breast. He saw her eyes close, her lips part. 'You wanted to talk about generators,' he managed unsteadily. 'I'm trying. We use permanent magnet motors.'

Somehow she overcame the barrier of his buttons, pushed the shirt away from the male contours of his chest and tangled her fingers in the fine hairs.

'Tell me,' she began, but then she shook her head, drawing closer, needing his lips on hers again. When his fingers slipped beneath the sweater, tracing the soft heat of her midriff, she dissolved into trembling desire. It was as if her weakness gave him strength, for he reached down and swept her up into his arms, carrying her into the room, bending to lay her on the thick quilt that covered the bed. She sank into the softness.

'Maggie . . .' For a long moment he was silent, then he touched her. She was breathless, aching with need. He whispered harshly, 'If you want to stop, it's all right, Maggie.'

She would have spoken, but her throat was filled with some obstruction that—strangely—brought tears to her eyes. She reached up to him, touching his face, needing to be part of him. Then he was beside her, taking her into his arms gently, carefully, touching her lips with his. She kissed his cheek, the cool flesh of his neck.

'Michael,' she whispered, clutching at him, moving against him and feeling the dizzy, spinning contact between them.

'I want to make love to you,' he groaned. He removed her sweater slowly, then he touched her softly, tracing her outline from her throat to her waist, his hand returning to one rounded breast encased in a lacy bra. He rubbed his thumb across the erect nipple through the lace. She gasped, her eyes closing, her head rolling on the bedspread.

'Please, Michael,' she whispered, her hands seeking feverishly against his chest. He came closer. Touching, loving, making her tremble, then groan in his arms.

She needed, needed . . . Oh, it had never been like this! So close. So good. He touched , kissed her everywhere, pushing aside the barriers. The music throbbed in her veins, the world spinning in a red haze. Dizzying, spinning, she trembled in his arms, pressing herself closer. She was hardly aware of the small noises that came from her throat as he caressed her to wild need, hardly aware of the words he whispered, then groaned.

His arms grew tight, hard around her. He pulled her close. His eyes were like fire above her, his voice low and caressing.

'Your eyes are green, Maggie. Green fire. Burning.'

She reached up to explore the shadows and contours of his chest. A deep warmth surged within her, spreading, covering everything. 'Make love to me,' she whispered, her fingers threading through the hairs of his chest, the crisp curls drawing lines of fire along her palms.

His head was closer, his mouth closing on hers, his body entering hers, taking possession, taking her on a journey past the stars, where they shared a shuddering climax that left them both trembling and spent in each other's arms . . . and they slept, curled together.

She woke when the music stopped.

Earlier, in the shuddering aftermath of their shared ecstasy, the music had faded to silence. A long moment later, Michael had whispered, 'Don't go anywhere, darling. I'm going to put more music on.'

He had returned with the low sound of music behind him, and she had melted into his arms again, gladly surrendering to their shared ecstasy. Now, some time later, she was still cradled against his sleeping body.

In sleep, the firmness of his face was relaxed to a boyish smoothness. His eyelids were smooth and soft, covering those penetrating grey eyes. Seeing him like this, she felt an intimacy almost as intense as their love-making had been. He looked very young. She wanted to touch his face, but she didn't want to wake him. Not yet. She closed her eyes, let the sensations cover her.

His arm was lying across the curve of her hip, the pressure shifting as he breathed. Her thigh was resting against his. Her head was at his shoulder. She felt a curious fullness, peacefulness, as if her own restless energies had somehow been fulfilled and drained off.

If she opened her eyes again, she would see Michael filling her vision. In this instant, she could not imagine how she was going to get up and walk away from him. His hand tightened on her hip, and she opened her eyes to find him watching her.

'Hello,' she whispered.

'Hello, Maggie.' His gaze was gentle and warm. He lifted the hand from her hip, brushed fingers through the tumbled hair on her forehead, asked huskily, 'Did you know that you're a fantastic lady?' She shook her head numbly. She touched his face, her fingers exploring the planes of his jaw.

He brushed her lips softly with his. 'From the first time I saw you, I've been bewitched.'

'Bewitched?' she repeated, hanging on the word. She pushed herself a little away from him. She felt the panic rising inside her. Love was the word that had flashed into her mind as he spoke, but love was entrapment and sorrow. She had loved Dick, hadn't she? Shadows passed over her eyes. Memories.

His fingers combed through her hair. His lips curved in a smile as he watched her through half-closed lids. His hand moved down, along the curves of her shoulder, her breast, her waist.

'Maggie, I know you felt it, too. It was never like this for either of us before.' He drew her closer. She found herself wanting him again, despite the raw panic welling up inside.

'We can't,' she said unsteadily, her lips against his. 'I can't, Michael.' They could have an affair, but he was going to ask for more. It was in his eyes, his touch . . . and his voice.

'I want to marry you, Maggie.'

His words were like a shock of cold water. She jerked back, breathing quickly and feeling the adrenalin surging in her veins.

'Maggie . . .'

Dick. Long nights alone. Wondering . . . Worrying. Dixie, her eyes bewildered, staring at her father as he stumbled through the door. Years filled with broken promises. Trying to find something for Dixie to eat in the mornings. Trying to find money for the bills that seemed to keep coming. Trying to remember the love in the midst of all the pain and uncertainty.

'Let's get married,' Dick had said, grinning at her.

'No,' she said now, slowly, shivering in a draught of cool air, seeing Michael's face strangely unfocused in front of her. She brought her arms up to hug herself, for warmth. 'No. This isn't——We're not——'

'Maggie, come here.' He was reaching for her again, trying to trap her. 'Come and get warm, darling.' She shook her head, jerked away, unconscious of her nakedness until his eyes dropped to her full breasts. She thought he was going to touch her, but he said softly, 'Easy, Maggie,' and she shuddered, alone.

He reached for a blanket that had tumbled to the floor, then walked around the bed, approaching her slowly, as if she were a frightened wild thing. He covered her shoulders with the blanket.

She avoided looking at his lean nakedness as he moved about the room. She felt cold, shivering despite the blanket. Nerves. The panic seemed to have smothered her, made it impossible for her to speak. He came back to the bed, sat beside her, handed her a glass filled with amber liquid.

'Try this,' he said softly. 'I don't really know if it will help, but it's the only thing around.' She got one hand outside the blanket and took the glass, sipping, feeling the cool liquid flowing down her throat.

Michael said, his voice very matter-of-fact, 'I've never asked a woman to marry me before. I wasn't prepared for you to go into shock.'

She giggled with nervousness verging on hysteria. The liquid in her glass sloshed. A little spilled on her wrist. 'Oh, Michael! I don't think this was a very good idea.'

He brushed the curls back from her cheek. 'Maggie——'

'They won't stay,' she said, talking about the curls.

'I know. But I enjoy touching your hair. Not just your hair, mind you. I like touching all of you.' Her body quivered, as if his words were his hands.

She said abruptly, 'We can't possibly get married.'

'Why not?'

She met his eyes. They weren't quite as soft any more. There was a certain tenderness mixed with something that made her nervous. As if he were embarked on a battle he meant to win. He might win their battle for Angus, but not this one.

She said sternly, 'It's not as simple as that.'

'Maggie, with you I know nothing is going to be simple. Exciting and wonderful, but not simple.' His voice changed, became brisk. 'Get dressed, darling. I'll take you home.' He stood up and pulled his trousers on. She tried not to look.

What kind of a woman was she? Torn between asking him to make love to her again—once more. Just once more. Because it might be the last time. Torn between that, and running away.

She shed the blanket, moved around the room, finding the clothing that had seemed a barrier only hours ago. She felt weak, as if he could call and she would come, re gardless of reason or will.

He wanted marriage. She shivered as the word echoed in her mind with the memories. Then she combed her hair and applied lipstick as straight as she could. She felt as if she had a wall around herself, insulating her from Michael.

'A taxi?' he asked as he shut the door of the room behind them. She shook her head.

'I can walk. I want to walk.' She was ahead of him, her face averted. She said brightly, 'You don't need to see me home. I often walk it on my own.'

He ignored that, and they were both silent as they left the hotel. Maggie did not recognise the desk clerk as they passed through the foyer, and she hoped she wasn't recognised either. Tonight would be easier to forget if Michael's name did not turn up on the lips of her friends.

When Michael reached for her hand, she found herself giving it, but she said, 'I'm not ready to get married again.' He said nothing and she added, 'I mean, I know we—tonight was——'

'Very special?' he suggested softly, his fingers curling around hers.

'Yes,' she admitted huskily, 'but——'

'But you're not ready for marriage?'

'That's it,' she agreed, relieved.

'So we'll take it a bit slower.' Michael tried to feel as patient as he sounded. As if he were negotiating with Rory Pederson. Rory wasn't keen to be taken over, either, but Michael thought he could win them both over, given time. He said carefully, 'I don't want to be away from you, Maggie.'

He had wanted her from that first day. Until tonight, he had believed that making love to her would free him, that he could go home alone and forget her once he had possessed her. That was what he had believed, but it was not true.

Maggie was addictive, and he knew now that he would never have enough of her. If he walked away from her now, he was likely to spend the rest of his life wondering if some other man were kissing her, trying to make love to her.

In between the streetlights was an area where darkness enfolded them. He could hardly see her, but he reached for her, needing to feel her close again. She came willingly into his arms, meeting his lips with her own in a breathlessly sweet kiss. He knew then that it would be all right, that despite what she said she would be his. He was going to win.

He let her go unwillingly, groaning, 'Maggie, when I go home, I'm going to miss you like hell!' His hands rubbed up and down her arms, as if he could feel her through the jacket and sweater. 'I'm going to be reaching for you, and you won't be there.'

She said nothing, but her lips were parted and trembling. 'Come with me, Maggie. No, don't say anything yet. I know you can't, not right away. But think about it. I've got a big house, with lots of room for you and Dixie both.' He took her lips deeply, plundered the sweet depths of her mouth. When she was clinging to him, her arms wound tightly around his neck, he urged her softly, 'Come live with me. Take your time deciding about marriage if you want, but meanwhile—come and live with me.'

She gasped and pulled away. 'I—I don't want to get married. Not——No! You can't just kiss me and I'll change my tune. I'm not a——I can't leave! I've got a job!'

'Leave it,' he said impatiently. 'Resign.'

Maggie shuddered. He sounded so reasonable, as if she were the one who was not making sense. 'I don't think you're taking me seriously, Michael. It's a game you're playing. You want me and——'

'Not just me, Maggie.' His voice was suddenly harsh on the salt air. 'I wasn't the only one.'

'No,' she admitted, her voice rising. 'It wasn't just you. But you're used to getting what you want, and it doesn't occur to you that I might not want to marry a man who sees me as part of his game plan!'

His hand was painfully hard on her arm. 'What the hell do you mean by that?'

'It's what you do, isn't it? What about that company you're trying to buy? You're in the middle of a takeover, aren't you? Why? What are you going to do that the owners wouldn't do with it?'

'Make it bigger, more successful.' He dropped her arm and she pulled away from him, rubbing the bruised skin.

Her voice dropped, revealing more than she wanted. 'Michael, the whole thing makes me feel—very vulnerable. As if you're planning on making me do something I don't want to do.' She concentrated on the light in a warehouse window up ahead. She started walking again, because that way she'd get home quicker, get the door shut on him. 'I wish you'd go away. Go and leave me alone.'

He kept pace as he said reasonably, 'Maggie, I can't. It was too late the first time I met you.'

This couldn't be real. Didn't the man know the meaning of the word *no*? He said, 'You're going to marry me,' as if he knew the future without doubt.

'I don't want to be apart from you. I don't think you want to be away from me, either. How long do you need? How much notice do you have to give. A month?'

Mechanically, exploring his proposition with unwilling fascination, she asked, 'What about Angus?'

'He can come, too.'

'You've got it worked out, have you?' His steps paced hers as her stride quickened with her agitation. 'Is this part of the battle for Angus? A way to get your dad down there?'

He said sharply, 'Don't be ridiculous!'

She shook her head, felt the curls tumbling around her face, welcoming the fury. 'You're damn right it's ridiculous! You and me? It's the craziest thing I ever heard of !' He didn't say anything, but she was shouting loud enough for both of them. 'Michael, I'm not leaving my job!' She came to the corner, turned left without looking for cars.

'Why not, Maggie? It's not that much of a job.' He sounded so calm and reasonable that her anger grew with every word he said. As if he were comparing magazine prices, he said, 'It can't pay all that well. I can certainly look after you and Dixie far better than you can on what you're making.' He fell silent abruptly, sensing his mistake.

She swung around to face him, her chest rising and falling quickly with her shallow, furious breaths. 'Dixie and I are doing just fine! We don't need you! We don't need anyone! I've been looking after her alone for six years—and before that I had my fill of being lied to and promised to and abandoned! I don't need a marriage. I damned well don't need a shack-up either!'

She looked around desperately. There was no escape except the railroad track a few steps farther down the hill, the waterfront road. Not another soul in sight. Just she and Michael, alone in the world, and she could feel the violence in him long seconds before he grabbed her, pulling her close.

'You're afraid, Maggie.' His voice was tight and hard, his hands rigid on her. 'That's it, isn't it?'

She twisted away. 'No! There's nothing between us. Just——'

'Nothing?' he challenged, his hands softening, stroking weakness into her bones. 'Why do you melt whenever you let yourself stay in my arms for more than a minute? Do you call that nothing? A night in each other's arms? Are you trying to tell me that's all it was?'

'Stop——' Her anger and his sensuous touch were boiling together into an explosive desire.

He shook his head roughly. 'Darling, you're dodging the issue, taking refuge in anger, but I'm not going to accept that.' He came closer, his shadow large against the sky. 'There's something between us, all right, and there's also something *standing* between us. I think it's time you told me about that husband of yours.'

She panicked. She knew she couldn't hold out against him for long. Not when his voice softened and said, 'We're what's important, Maggie. You and I. Our relationship.'

She denied it furiously. 'We don't have a relationship. We have—had an affair. A very brief one, because it isn't going to happen again. I hardly know you, and you're leaving tomorrow—no, today. That's the end of it.'

She stared at him without sight, and it was a long moment before she realised that his arms weren't stopping her from walking on. There was just his voice following, demanding, 'Are you still in love with him?'

She shivered. Dick was the biggest failure in her life. For all his declarations of love, she had never meant enough to him to stop his drinking or his playing around with other women. Even in the beginning, it had been wrong. If she had not become pregnant shortly after their marriage, she doubted the marriage would have lasted a year. The relationship, as far as she could see in retrospect, had supplied few of his needs and none of hers. She was better alone.

She didn't realise that she'd stopped walking until Michael took her shoulders between his hands, shaking her slightly from behind. When he touched her, she had trouble making herself pull away. Behind her, his voice sounded rough and gravelly. 'Is he that important, that you can't even talk about him?'

She tossed back her hair, shaking memories away, or trying to. She wished she didn't feel so exposed by Michael's questions. She was afraid he would ask too much, delve too deep, and she would lose the mask that protected her from hurt.

'Does it bother you?' she asked tightly, gathering strength by attacking him. 'Does it hurt your male ego to think I might still want him after having you?'

'God damn it, Maggie! That's garbage and you know it!' He dropped his hands from her as if she'd burned him.

'Is it? Then why are you trying to get me to talk about Dick? You're jealous!' When she swung to confront him, she found him looking away.

He said tightly, his jaw rigid, 'Jealous? Of course I'm jealous. Not that I give a damn about what went before, but when it interferes with now—with you and me—then yes, I'm, jealous! If you're in my arms, and you're remembering him, then I'm damned well jealous!'

She couldn't bear to stand there, exposed, in front of him. She turned away and started walking quickly, but he was beside her, keeping pace. 'Don't run away from me, Maggie. You can't walk away from this. We've got to work it out.'

She took a deep, ragged breath, fighting the pull of his will. 'Michael, you're treating me like—a—— Oh, God! I don't want to get into this!'

'Go ahead Maggie, say it. What is it that stops you? Is it Dick?'

'I—I don't want to get into something like that again. You want——' He wanted to use her for his own needs, not for hers. 'You want me to come south, quit my job, live with you. For what?' The anger was easier now. 'What are you going to give me in return? I'm supposed to give up everything. My career—you might not think much of my job, but I love it! It's our security—mine and Dixie's. What am I to do down there in Victoria? Take the place vacated by your ex-roommate?'

'Maggie——' He stopped himself from hasty words, tried to understand what was really behind her fears. 'If it's Sam that's bothering you, you don't need to——'

'No, I don't need to be jealous of her, do I?' She stopped walking, faced him with her voice flaming, her hands settling aggressively on her hips. 'I suppose she was a nice woman, and you cast her off pretty easily, didn't you? I can see that Sam's turn is over. It's my turn now, isn't it? Sure, that's it! Move Maggie in and—— How long will it be, Michael? After all, you don't exactly have a good track record. Mine's better. I stayed with my husband for five years, and that's a hell of a lot more stable a relationship than yours was!' She shuddered. Stable? What on earth was she saying?

He was watching her as if she were a corporate piece to be manoeuvred in a takeover bid. He asked, 'Are you afraid I'll stop wanting you?'

'No, damn it!' She hugged herself tightly. 'Yes! No, it's everything! It's not—I don't want anything from you! And you can't have anything from me!'

'You already gave me something,' he said softly.

'Stop twisting my words! Stop analysing what I say as if it were——'

He moved closer, his lips brushing her cheek as he

murmured, 'Someone's got to be rational, darling. You're far too emotional for it to be you, so it had better be me, or we won't get anywhere.'

'You bastard! You . . . Oh, damn! Damn!' She was terrified that he would pull her into his insane proposition against her will. 'Will you please leave me alone? Get out of here! Go back to the bloody hotel and let me have some peace from this!'

'No, Maggie. I'm not leaving you in the middle of a fight. We've got to come to some sort of agreement.'

'Agreement?' Her voice squeaked. 'You mean, you expect me to say yes to you? Tonight? Is that what you expect?'

She felt dizzy from the force of her own emotions. She was glad of the dark that surrounded them. 'Isn't it a bit confusing, Mickey? Being involved in two takeover bids at once? You're after that motor company in Vancouver. And me.'

He sounded as if he were smiling. 'Compared to you, Maggie, Pederson's is a cinch.'

She would not let herself smile back. She got her voice down, though, to a cold crispness that sounded businesslike enough. 'How does it go, Michael? Proposal and counterproposal?'

'Sometimes,' he agreed.

She thought he sounded uncomfortable with the new direction she had given their conversation. She nodded. 'I thought it might. You've made a proposal. Marriage, wasn't it? Pretty high stakes, it seems to me, considering you've only known me a few weeks. I refused, and you suggested a lower level takeover. I should move in with you, as sort of a non-status lover?' She was trying to break that calm. She listened for a sign of anger, because she believed she could best an angry Michael. It was his cool control that defeated her.

He pushed his hands into his pockets, said very casually, 'Not the wording I would choose, but essentially correct.'

She nodded. 'Yes, I thought I had kept track of the negotiations pretty well. So it's my turn for a counter-proposal, I think. It's quite simple. Since I won't quit my job, and I don't want to move—well, I can hardly move without quitting my job, can I?—there's only one solution if you really want me. You do want me, don't you?'

What on earth was she doing? He was very quiet, his silhouette frozen. She was suddenly nervous that the coolness was only skin-deep, that inside something was boiling up in him, getting out of control. She knew she should stop, but the words kept coming. 'How much do you want me? Enough to respect my way of life? My job? My home? Do you, Michael? If you want me that badly, you'll have to give up your job. Get rid of your business and come north. You can move in with me.'

She realised suddenly that he could turn her words into an offer that would entangle her in goodness knew what kind of situation. He was the man who knew how to turn anything to his advantage, and she was the girl who talked before she thought.

But he was too angry to see the advantage she had given him. 'Maggie, you talk about me playing games, but really it's your speciality, isn't it? You're an honest, forthright girl, but when anyone tries to come close, you're a little hell-cat, aren't you?' He laughed, but it sounded terrible to her ears. She stepped back. That seemed to amuse him even more. 'Afraid I'll force myself on you again, Maggie? What is it you're protecting with your games? Your wonderful life? It's great, isn't it? You're so lonely, you're hanging tight on to an old man who's too old to live this life any more.'

She shook her head mutely, but he went on, his voice growing hard and angry, 'That was your real reason for fighting me when I came to bring Angus home, wasn't it? But you shouldn't worry, Maggie.' She heard the bitterness, realised that somehow she had injured him. 'If my father leaves, you'll have sole possession of the last finger of Rushbrooke floats. I can see that's a prize worth having. Your little empire, where no one threatens you, no one asks anything of you except a smile and a berth. What will it be like for you ten years from now, Maggie? You'll be nearing forty then. A middle-aged lady with a smile and an empty heart.'

No, it wouldn't be the way he said. There was more in her life, people she cared about. Surely there didn't have to be a man in her bed? She had Dixie and Angus, Darryl and Jan and . . .

'Dixie will be gone then,' he went on in a deceptively soft voice. 'She'll be living her own life, not with her mother any more. And my father will be gone because, whatever you think, however you fight, he's not going to be living on the docks much longer either. Just Maggie. All alone.'

She shivered, staring at him, trying desperately to find words to throw back before he realised what he was doing to her. She wasn't sure why she should cry, because they were only words, and he was only a man she'd known for a couple of weeks—but she was blinking to keep the tears from falling, and in her throat there was a lump that wouldn't subside. She hardly heard the sound of a car approaching slowly behind her. Michael reached a hand towards her and she stepped back, shaking her head mutely. She wanted to get away, but he kept coming after her.

'Maggie, come here.'

'Please go away.' Her voice was filled with distress.

She could feel tears overflowing on to her cheeks. 'Leave me alone, Mickey.'

'Maggie, I'm sorry.' He touched her, but she jerked away. 'Maggie, I—I don't know what got into me.'

She shook her head. 'Go away, Mickey. Let me be.'

'Maggie, I——' She wouldn't let him touch her. He tried to make her smile, saying, 'This isn't the kind of behaviour that would win me any business deals. I—I didn't mean to say any of that. Maggie . . .'

She shook her head wordlessly. Behind her, the wheels crunched, and a voice said, 'Good evening. Everything all right here?'

Michael muttered something under his breath, then said, 'Fine. We're just out for a walk.' Maggie swung around and found herself looking down into the curious face of Herb, a young RCMP officer she knew from her job.

'Maggie!' The officer's voice was startled. He glanced at Michael, put a question into his voice as he said, 'I guess everything's fine? I'm just patrolling down this way. Any problems down at the floats lately, Maggie?'

She brushed an arm over her face, hoped neither man realised she was wiping away tears. She glanced back at Michael, said in a strained voice, 'Herb, this is Michael MacAvoy. He was just walking me home, but if you're going that way, I'd appreciate a ride.'

It seemed like providence. A ready-made escape.

CHAPTER EIGHT

MAGGIE found herself lying in her bed alone every night, listening to the sound of Dixie's breathing, trying not to think about Michael. It had been a mistake, letting him make love to her. She had assumed that she was a modern woman, able to handle a casual affair—but now she was dreaming of his touch and his voice, even having visions of him sitting at her breakfast table in the mornings!

He was the first lover she had taken in all the years since Dick. Why did he have to make all those demands? Marriage. Quitting her job. As if possessing her just once meant he owned her! She shivered, feeling a coldness that wasn't there, remembering angry, painful words spoken in the darkness.

Michael had predicted that Dixie would go and she would be left alone. Of course the years would pass, and her daughter would grow up, but Maggie would be ready for that when the time came. Michael had no idea what he was talking about!

She was exhausted in the mornings after the sleepless nights. She knew that Angus was watching her. Did he know she and Michael had become lovers? He looked tired, too. Several times he mentioned the coming winter. She thought of his boat, the diesel heater that wasn't going to be enough for him when the winter winds blew. Before winter, she was certain that Michael would somehow manage to move Angus south. The old man had been living next to her for years, and Maggie knew that she was going to miss him terribly.

Her world seemed to be going insane, everyone behaving oddly. They said people behaved strangely at the full moon, and maybe it was true. The feud between Solly and Rex exploded, with Solly pounding his fists on Rex's boat, threatening again to kill the dog. Then, the next day, Rex talking to the police because someone had stolen Solly's dinghy and Solly insisted it was Rex. For the first time, Maggie felt as if it were all too much for her. Solly and Rex would probably kill each other, and she would be in the middle when the shooting started.

At home she had troubles, too. Dixie was wound up and ready to fight about everything and anything. Maggie found herself shouting back at her daughter almost every evening. She seemed totally out of hand.

On Wednesday night Dixie breezed home from school and announced that she had met a new friend—Holly—and wanted to spend the night. Maggie forbade her to go out. It was a school night, and Dixie must have homework to do. She had not done any homework all week.

'I'm going anyway, no matter what you say!' Dixie had screamed before she slammed out of the door.

Maggie spent hours not knowing where Dixie was, worried sick. Several times she ran up to the office on the wharf, using the harbour's board telephone to call all Dixie's friends in hopes of some hint as to who Holly was, where she lived. What had got into Dixie? Once Maggie might have turned to Angus for advice, but these days her neighbour seemed too frail to take on another burden.

Finally, some time after dark, when Maggie had just called the hospital and the police, Dixie walked through the front door, silent and sulking.

She refused to tell Maggie where she had been.

'It's my life! It's none of your business!' the girl

screamed. After a long verbal battle, they both went to their beds for the night. Neither of them slept well.

At breakfast the next morning, Dixie still seemed resentful and subdued. Maggie knew she should say something, but had no idea what. Hopefully, a day away from Dixie would result in her being able to think more clearly, to formulate some plan of action in dealing with her suddenly rebellious daughter.

Just after Dixie left for school, Maggie found a workman on her doorstep.

'City telephone,' he announced cheerful. 'You're the wharfinger, aren't you?'

'Yes,' she agreed warily. Vandalism was a recurring problem on the poorly lit waterfront road, and it was only a month since the last time they had lost their telephone service to vandals.

'I'm here to install your phone. I've got to check with the wharfinger on where to run the wires, 'n you're the wharfinger. So I'm here to ask you where to run the wires.'

He didn't look like a crazy man, but she couldn't make any sense of it. 'What phone?' she asked.

He waved a clipboard. 'Your name's Simpson?'

'Yes, but——' She wondered who at the telephone office could have messed up the paperwork this badly. 'I can't get a telephone down here. I've tried.'

Angus stepped into *Sasha's* cockpit. He was listening, and later they would have a laugh about this crazy telephone man.

The telephone man said patiently, 'Yes, you can. I'm here to put it in.'

Maggie rubbed her temple where she could feel the headache coming on. 'You—I didn't ask for a telephone.' She shook her head and corrected herself. 'Well, I did, but that was years ago. They told me it was impossible, you couldn't run the wires all the way out here.'

His smile was becoming strained, and Maggie had the feeling that he had stereotyped her as a crazy, difficult female. 'You can get the wires run anywhere you want, if you'll pay for it. Well, anywhere the electrical code permits.' He pointed back towards the main wharf and said, 'I'd suggest we run them up in the air, from piling to piling, to avoid any problem with the floats moving on the tide. If that's all right with Fisheries and Oceans, I'll get on with it.'

'Pay? I can't *pay*!' The state her bank account was in now, she could not afford even to think about the new shoes she needed. She said unequivocally, 'Look, I don't know how you got here, or why you've come now, but you'll have to go right back where you came from!'

He lifted the clipboard as if he wished he could use it as a weapon. She felt a sudden urge to get into a slanging match with him as he said tensely, 'Look, lady, don't mess up my day! The order is right here. See! It says "paid", so whether you remember or not, you've paid the money and now I'm here to put in your flaming telephone! So why don't you just tell me if it's OK to run the wires across the pilings, and where you want the phone inside, and I'll get on with it.'

She didn't understand any of it, but if he wanted to give her a telephone, she would take it. Later, she could have the joy of telling them to take the damned thing back out again!

'I'm going insane,' she told Angus, but he was smiling. She tossed back her hair as if the feel of wind on her face might clear her brain. 'Where did this telephone come from? Can you tell me that?'

Angus didn't realise it was a rhetorical question. He said simply, 'Mickey, of course. Where else?' Maggie stared at him wordlessly. Angus was grinning at her, saying, 'It's the kind of thing he'd do. He wants to be able to talk to you, and you've got no phone. So—I won't walk the rest of the way with you, Maggie. I'm a bit stiff this morning.'

'Michael?' She was almost screaming. 'You mean, he went down to the telephone office and—— No, he can't take over my life like that! I don't need looking after or paying for or——' Angus looked terribly tired suddenly. Her anger died abruptly. 'Are you feeling all right?'

He nodded and turned to look back at his boat. 'Getting older, that's all. *Sasha's* been good to me, but it's time I moved ashore.'

Maggie swallowed a lump in her throat. 'You're leaving?'

'Yes, before winter comes. I think I'll go to Mickey.' Then he grinned. 'Or maybe I'll go to Heather. That'd shake her!'

'I'll miss you.' There didn't seem anything else to say. She could feel Michael's prophecy coming true. Everybody around her leaving, and Maggie left alone.

Angus asked suddenly, 'Are you angry at Mickey?'

Maggie rubbed her forehead. It was going to be a terrible headache. She said dully, 'I don't know what I feel.' He looked worried, and she had no idea how to reassure him.

'He's a good boy, Maggie. He's got a good heart.'

She was incredulous. 'A good boy? He's trying to take me over!'

Angus shrugged and hunched his shoulders against a light wind that was twisting around the boats. 'You'll just have to keep him in line.'

Maggie swallowed. 'I thought Mickey had the market on preposterous statements. You talk as if we—as if Michael and I were——' She felt the flush spreading over her cheeks. 'As if—just because——' He knew that they had spent a night together. She saw the knowledge in his eyes and she felt as self-conscious as a young girl.

She fled both Angus and the wharfs. She shut herself into the trailer, dealing with the paperwork that she usually put off until the last moment. She stared at the mess of papers, knowing that somehow she had to get her mind straightened out. She was walking around in a daze, letting everything get out of control. When the telephone rang, she jerked a dark line across the September moorage sheet before she reached for the receiver.

'It's the attendance clerk at Seal Cove school, Mrs Simpson. I tried to contact you yesterday, but there was no answer. Dixie wasn't at school yesterday afternoon. Was she home sick?'

Maggie hesitated, taken by surprise. Her first instinct was to protect Dixie, but she resisted, deciding that Dixie must take the consequences for her behaviour. Dixie had gone to school yesterday. If she had not arrived, then she must have played truant. Why? As far as Maggie knew, she had never done anything like that before. Was it Holly, the new friend?

How on earth was she supposed to handle this? Should she punish Dixie? Talk to her? For the first time, she felt a real sympathy for her own father's dilemma in bringing up the teenage Maggie.

When the telephone rang again, she picked it up absently, her mind on Dixie.

'Good morning, darling,' said a warm, husky voice.

'Michael?' She closed her eyes, saw his face clearly in front of her. She had been hungering for the sound of his voice. She wanted to feel angry with him, but she was terribly glad to hear his voice. 'Where are you?'

'At work.' With her eyes closed, she could see him clearly. When she heard his voice, she had had a crazy fantasy that he was calling from the airport here in Prince Rupert. She tried to imagine his office. Comfortable, she thought. Well organised. 'What can you see out of your window?' she asked breathlessly.

'Another building. Cars, if I look down.' There was a smile in his voice. 'What about you? What can you see out off your window?'

'Boats,' she said automatically. Outside, a man walked past the window and she added, 'And a man from the telephone company.'

'Good.' He sounded pleased with himself. 'I keep phoning the number—your new number, but it's not in service yet.'

She took her pen and drew a happy face on next month's moorage sheet, then she scrubbed it out angrily. 'Michael, you had no right to arrange that telephone . . .' As she spoke, the door to the trailer opened. Rex came in and leaned heavily on the counter. Maggie glared at him, wishing he would go away.

In her ear, Michael said, 'I wanted to talk to you.'

Rex was drumming his fingers on the counter, looking out of the door, impatience radiating from him. 'Michael, I've got to go. There's someone here.'

'I'll wait,' he said, as if he had all the time in the world. Rex strode to the door and looked out, then swung back into the trailer. The low voice in her ear said, 'Go ahead, darling. Deal with it, then come back to me. I'll wait.'

She put the receiver down on the desk. He was going to be hard to forget. Harder than the fisherman, or the doctor, or even Dick, who had been her husband for years. Even the sound of his voice filled her with a drugging mixture of warmth and need.

She stared blankly at Rex and he glared back at her. 'Maggie, figure out my moorage and I'll pay up. I'm getting the hell out of here! Today!' With his shaggy hair everywhere and his eyes flashing anger, he looked like a wild man.

She could not seem to focus on Rex. She picked up the moorage book, started flipping through the pages. Would Michael really wait? Did she want him to wait? She knew it would be best if she had the telephone taken out, refused this gift that could so easily entrap her.

Rex pounded the counter, tossing his head and sending the wild hair flying. 'That son of a seahorse! He thinks he can get away with anything, but this is one bloody thing too much! I'm going to clean that bastard's clock!'

Maggie pushed the big book on to the counter between them. She might have felt nervous of Rex's sudden rage, but Michael, waiting on the telephone, gave her an irrational feeling of security. 'You owe for August, Rex, and eighteen days in September.'

He pounded the counter again, leaving a faint impression in the open pages of the moorage book. 'He's suing me! Can you believe that, Maggie? He's suing me! And he's suing my dog!'

She fought a terrible urge to giggle. If Michael could hear, he must be laughing. She pulled the calculator towards herself and started punching in numbers. 'I'll tell you what you owe in a minute. Where are you taking your boat?'

'Fairview terminal,' he said explosively, swinging away to the doorway again, coming back with his wallet out.

When he was gone, she didn't even put away the moorage book before she went back to the telephone. 'Are you still there?' she asked breathlessly.

'Yes, Maggie.' His voice was warm in her ear. 'I'd give anything to be in the court when that case comes up.'

She giggled, her thumb moving on the receiver as if he could feel the caress. 'Can you sue a dog?'

'I don't know, but I pity the poor judge when those two get into a courtroom together!' She believed she could see the lines that appeared at the corners of his eyes when he laughed.

'Michael, I miss you.' She hadn't known she was going to say that. Her fingers tightened on the receiver until they hurt. She wished she could retrieve her words.

'Maggie.' His voice was husky. He cleared his throat. 'Maggie, when I go home at night, I—it seems so empty. A house without you in it.' She swallowed. Angus had told her about the house. He and Sasha had lived there all their married life. It was a house of love, and Michael was alone there.

'Michael——'

'I want you with me, darling.'

The telephone man's feet appeared as he climbed down the pole outside her window. He started down the ramp with a big coil of wire.

'Maggie?' The radio on her desk crackled. Michael said, 'You want to be with me, too, don't you, Maggie?'

The pen in her hand was making doodles on a piece of paper. 'We can't, it's impossible.' Something welled up and almost smothered her voice. 'I've got to go.'

'First tell me you love me.' His voice seemed to penetrate through to her core. At her elbow, the radio blared aggressively.

'Tell me,' he insisted.

'No,' she whispered.

His demand echoed through her all day long, and she kept denying it. She did not love him. No, it was too much. He could not expect her to pack up and set off into the unknown. Well, maybe it was ridiculous calling

Victoria the unknown, but why should she give everything up? Her job. Her home.

He would expect her to be like Sam. Had Sam given dinner parties for him? Maggie had never given a dinner party in her life. She didn't know what you cooked or what you said to the guests, and she did not want to know!

She pushed Michael out of her thoughts, concentrated on worrying why Dixie was so late getting home from school that night. When she finally arrived, walking slowly along the floats, Maggie stopped her.

'I've got to talk to you.'

Dixie shrugged. 'Is Grandpa Angus coming to dinner tonight?'

Maggie shook her head, refusing to be distracted. 'You missed school yesterday.'

'I never did! I——' She broke off her denial and stared at her mother resentfully.

Maggie wished Dixie didn't look so sullen. This wasn't going to go easily. 'Honey, don't lie. They phoned me from the school today. Where were you?' The girl shrugged. 'Dixie——'

'I was out for a walk, that's all!' She flung her curls around her head in an angry tangle, and ran away towards the house. When Maggie followed her, she found the bedroom door closed and Dixie on the other side.

Maggie stared at the closed door, worried and yet unsure whether this was something serious going on with Dixie, or a stage that would blow over with time.

If only she had someone to lean on, to turn to with the problems that were too much for her. For a time, she had thought of Angus as someone she could lean on, although in fact he had leaned on her more than the other way around.

She closed her eyes, an uncalled vision of Michael

washing over her. When the telephone rang, she picked it up with a jerk. There was no one it could be, except Michael.

'You sound tired,' he said, and her fingers trembled on the receiver.

'It was a long day,' she evaded.

'Did Rex get away?' She could hear music around his voice, the same soft music he had played the night they made love.

'Yes.' She pulled absently at a thread that was coming out of the upholstery, and said, 'Solly stood on the wharf and watched him go, muttering threats. There's already another boat in Rex's space.'

Michael said, 'Let's hope he doesn't have a dog.'

She giggled. 'Oh, let's hope not!' She curled her legs up on the sofa and closed her eyes so she could see him better. What harm could this do? Just a conversation in the dark. She would have liked to tell him about Dixie, to share the worry, but it would do no good to lean on him when she would be alone in the end. In any case, Dixie could easily be awake in the next room, listening. 'What about you?' she asked. 'What did you do today? Tell me.'

He was not in the habit of talking about his work, but he started telling her about an idea he had for a new twelve-volt metering system. She asked him questions, and found that she could understand his explanations. She thought he would make a good teacher, and she told him so.

'Actually, I thought of that once,' he admitted, sounding almost shy. 'I almost applied for a job teaching at a community college.'

'Why didn't you?' The fingers of her free hand were stroking the arm of the sofa. She wondered what he was wearing.

'Dad asked me to come into the business. He wanted help and, well, it sort of caught me up after that.'

If she opened her eyes, he would be there, looking at her. 'And you've never looked back?' she asked him, smiling, knowing he liked her smile.

'Sometimes,' he admitted. 'But there's no point, is there? I'm here, and there are aspects of it that I like.'

'Playing with electronic circuits? Trying to take over Pederson Motors? That seems like such a contradiction, yet both those things are you, aren't they?'

Outside, there was a wind blowing. She opened her eyes and felt a painful sense of loss because the chair across from her was empty. She must be insane, enjoying his voice when she knew she must send him away. She really could not handle the emotional upheaval of another serious relationship, and she was crazy to be thinking she could handle even an affair with this man.

He said, 'I don't get the time to play with many electronic circuits these days.'

'So you concentrate on the takeovers? What if Pederson doesn't want to be taken over?'

'He doesn't.' He sounded as if that didn't matter.

'Then why are you doing it?' The wind had loosened something on her roof. She heard the banging, hoped she wasn't going to lose more shingles. Last year she had developed innumerable leaks when the autumn storms came.

'I don't know,' said Michael, sounding surprised at his admission. 'The challenge, I guess. All the odds seem against getting Pederson to agree, so I can't resist trying to find a way.'

'Is that why you want me? Am I a challenge, Michael?'

'The biggest challenge, Maggie. The one I can't afford to lose.'

She felt an unwilling surge of excitement. It was a heady feeling, knowing that Michael MacAvoy was devoting much of his energies to trying to tempt Maggie Simpson into sharing her life with him.

'What do you plan next?' she asked huskily, intrigued against her will.

'Are you talking about Pederson? Or you?' It should have sounded like a joke, but his voice was very deep and she felt her heart pounding. The palms of her hands were damp. She knew that, if she stood, her legs would be trembling.

'Pederson,' she said, as if it were a game.

'I can't even think about Pederson these days. There's a picture of you painted on the back of my eyelids. Every time I close my eyes, it's only you I can see.'

'Then me,' she said, whispering. 'What are you planning for me?'

'I want to make love to you every night on the phone.' This was the voice that had loved her in the night. 'I'm going to make sure you don't forget me while I'm away from you, while I'm trying to think of how to get you to marry me. I want you to share your days with me. Every night I'm going to call you and find out all about your day.' She heard him take a deep, shaky breath. 'You said I plan things, and it's true. I'm planning this, and it had better work! I want to make you need me at the end of the day. I want you to come into that little house, and wait for the moment when I call you. All day, I want you to be thinking of it.'

'No,' she said sharply, then her voice somehow went on as if it had its own will, 'Dixie's been playing hookey from school.' She stared at her own fingers on the armchair, the cuff of her green shirtwaist blouse. 'Just once, I think. Yesterday.'

'Did you ask her why?' His voice was low and serious, as if he cared very much whether Dixie skipped school.

She shook her head, then realised he couldn't see. 'I—she said she'd gone for a walk.'

'Do you think she was telling the truth?' He sounded so rational, so calm. She wished he were here.

'I don't know. She's been funny lately.' She shifted restlessly in the chair, her voice echoing her worry, 'All week we've been fighting, at each other's throats. I'm sorry, this isn't what you called for, is it? It's my problem and——'

'If it's your problem, then it's mine, too.' His voice was very warm and caring. 'I can't get there until Saturday, Maggie, but I'll come Saturday afternoon. If you haven't got to the bottom of it by then, I'll try to talk to Dixie. If you need me before that, just call, sweetheart.'

She had to be able to stand alone. She could not let herself lean on him, need him. 'Michael, I ——'

'Don't worry, Maggie.'

She said abruptly, 'There's so many things you don't know about me. I'm a messy housekeeper, you know. No, don't laugh! When you get into a—a takeover bid, all you think about is winning. But you've got to realise that it really can't work.'

'It'll work.' It had to be arrogance, or insanity, for him to be that sure. 'I didn't pick you for your domestic talents. I know you're not the perfect housekeeper.'

'Your place is probably immaculate,' she said tightly. The coffee-table in front of her was strewn with magazines. She could see a spot on the kitchen floor where she'd spilled a few drops of coffee that morning and hadn't wiped it up yet.

'Tidy,' he agreed mildly. 'You should think of that in my favour. I pick up my own socks, and I'm even willing to do the vacuuming. And I can cook.'

'So can I,' she snapped, 'but I'm not looking for a man. And you're crazy to think I'm the woman for you.' But hearing his voice made it impossible for her to deny to herself how much she wanted to see him again. With a hint of desperation in her voice, she asked, 'Couldn't we just have an affair?'

'No, Maggie. An affair's not enough. Not for either of us.'

It had to be enough—or perhaps it was too much. Anything with this man was too much for her. Just listening to his voice, to his claim that her worries were his, too, had her wanting to turn to him and ask him to take all her problems, to look after her.

When he hung up, she sat for a long time with her eyes closed, feeling alone because he was not there, wanting him to come and take over her problem with Dixie. Then, finally, she opened her eyes and saw her own things around her.

Inside that desk was the letter Dick had written. Dick had spoken sweet words, too. He had said that he loved her, that he would look after her. He had taken her to the hospital when she was in labour with Dixie. She had been suddenly afraid of the delivery ahead, and she had clung to him as she went into the emergency entrance, unwilling to be parted by the routine of her admission.

That was the last she had seen of him for a week. When she had come out of the delivery room after having Dixie, he had not been there. In the days that followed he did not visit her. She had no idea where he was, and he did not reappear through all the days of her hospitalisation.

She had taken the new baby home, frightened and holding the tiny Dixie bundled in the baby shawl she had knitted during the months of her pregnancy. At home, in the small apartment, there had been no sign of him. The two rooms had been cold, the electricity turned off—for non-payment of the bill, she supposed, although she had not seen the warning notice.

She had no resources to support her child, no way of making a living. She was trained for nothing and she had nothing. In her arms, Dixie was crying from the cold. Soon, she would be hungry, and although Maggie could nurse her she must eat well herself to feed her baby.

Dick had married her with promises that he would look after her. She had left the university, herself totally untrained for any work, and she had let herself become dependent on him. He had given her the child and now he was gone.

When the telephone rang, it was the hotel where he worked, giving her an angry message for Dick if he ever returned. He was fired.

Alone, she would never have called on her parents for help, but the new baby was more important than her pride. She picked up the telephone, dialled a desperate call home, only to find that there was no answer except an answering service announcing that her parents had gone for a week-long trip to Las Vegas.

Alone and helpless, she called a crisis line that was listed in the telephone book. Within hours the heat was back on in the apartment, and there was a selection of wholesome food in her cupboard, but it was only a temporary measure and she knew that she would have to find some way to support Dixie.

Two days later Dick returned, smiling sheepishly, filled with apologies and promises. 'I don't know what happened, Maggie. I just panicked, there in the hospital. I had to get out and have a drink. I promise you, honey, that it will never happen again. Never!'

At first she did not believe him. She told him she was

leaving him, but inside she was terrified, not knowing how she could manage to support herself and Dixie. Dick had cried when she threatened to leave him, insisting that he would never abandon her again.

For a time it seemed that things would be different. Within a week Dick had managed to get a job managing a small grocery store, with a free suite above the store thrown in for them to live in. Maggie concentrated on looking after Dixie, helping Dick get organised in his new job. After a while, she started to relax. Things were getting better, Dick was becoming more dependable, drinking less.

Dixie had helped, the baby bonding them together, making Dick a husband she could rely on. When six months had gone by without Dick disappearing or coming home drunk, she knew that it was going to be all right.

In fact, it was almost a year before he disappeared again.

If only marriage were like it was in the books; but it had never been true, not from the beginning.

CHAPTER NINE

MICHAEL arrived late on Saturday afternoon, just in time to share supper with them. Knowing he was coming, Maggie had invited Angus to supper. She felt the need of other people around, to act as barriers to any plans he might have for being alone with her.

All through supper she kept up a bright chatter, avoiding any personal topic, filling Michael in on all sorts of details about waterfront life that he probably did not want to hear.

When the supper dishes were cleared from the table, she followed Angus into the kitchen, saying, 'You and I will wash up, shall we, Angus?'

Michael made no protest, but to Maggie he looked as if he had everything planned out in advance. He turned to Dixie, saying casually, 'How about your taking me for a walk, Dixie?'

Dixie agreed eagerly, as if she wanted nothing more than to get outside. Maggie knew that he would be back, that he was merely biding his time until later, when it would be harder for her to avoid being alone with him.

All the time they were gone, she was trying to work out how to ask Angus to stay, not to leave her alone with Michael. In the end she could not think of any way that would not worry Angus.

She had no idea what went on between Dixie and Michael on their walk, but Dixie returned very quiet and subdued, then played three games of draughts with Michael, lost two of them, and announced that she was going to bed early.

156

Maggie followed her into the bedroom but, although Dixie allowed herself to be kissed goodnight, she seemed very sombre and immediately curled up tightly under the covers, facing towards the wall. Maggie wanted to ask about Dixie's walk with Michael, but she was afraid that Dixie would be angry at her intrusion. She had better leave well enough alone. Right now, at least the girl seemed to have got over the sulky anger she had displayed all week.

Back in the living-room, Maggie found Michael alone. 'Where's Angus?' she asked nervously.

'Gone home to bed.' He was wearing trousers that might be the ones he had worn the first time she saw him. Above them, he had on a silk shirt and a soft sweater that she knew would feel wonderful against her cheek. His eyes seemed to be burning as they watched her. She moved slowly towards him, let him take her hands in his and draw her down beside him on the sofa.

'Dixie,' she said as he bent his head and touched her forehead with his lips. 'She's awake.'

'She'll have to get used to it.' His lips explored the soft flesh around her eyes. 'After all, other girls' parents must kiss each other.'

She shook her head. 'Michael, this has got to stop. We can't possibly have any kind of relationship. I can't——'

His lips found hers and she couldn't say anything at all. His arms were around her, smoothing her curves against him until she was lying held against his chest, her face turned to his, accepting the intimacy of his lips, returning it with her own kisses, even while she knew how insane it was.

His throat was trembling, vulnerable under her fingertips. She felt the contours of his neck, slipped her fingers through his hair. Then his lips firmed, and she was pulling his head down, drawing herself up tight against

him, her breasts crushing against the softness of his
sweater, feeling the hard rigidity of his chest beneath.

He moulded the tension of her back, the gentle curve
of her waist, up to the swelling of her woman's breasts.
She felt a spasm go through her, taking the strength
from her arms, leaving her a trembling mass of pleasure
under his touch.

'I want to see you,' he groaned, his lips against her
throat, his fingers impatient on her clothing.

'We can't.' She groaned soundlessly as his thumb
found and stroked the hardness of a rigid nipple, gasped,
'I can't leave Dixie. Not tonight.'

She must somehow hold him away, not let him make
love to her again. Another night together and she would
be helpless against her own desires to beg him to take
her, hold her and keep her for ever.

For ever was a fairy-tale. The things he made her want
were real only in the story books, yet she could not seem to
prevent herself becoming soft and willing under his hands.
He shifted and she was lying down on the sofa, Michael
kneeling on the carpet beside her, bending over her.

'Michael . . .' Her heart was a slow, deep pulse that
seemed to shudder through her whole body, the very
centre of her being trembling with each heartbeat.

'You're going to marry me,' he whispered, his lips
tracing the thrust of her cheekbone, his teeth grasping
the lobe of her ear gently, his breath a hot tickle in her
ear. 'Then we can be together always.'

She felt a terrible panic as he talked of marriage. It was
as if he were trapping her, trying to drag her down to
that helpless, dependent degradation of her nightmares.

She made a faint motion that should have pulled her
free, but his fingers were drugging her will with soft
caresses, working open the buttons of her blouse.
'You're beautiful, Maggie,' he whispered. He touched

the lace at the top of her brief, uplifting bra. 'Did you wear that for me?'

'No,' she whispered. She could feel his eyes as if he were touching every part of her, then his fingers brushed the soft skin above the lace. Although she knew that she must not let him gain any more power over her, she could not seem to fight her own desire for his touch.

He bent to kiss the place where his fingers had been. 'I know we can't be alone tonight, but I had to see you, to touch you.' He found the front clasp of the bra, released it and let her breasts spring free of their confinement. She felt the air on her skin, closed her eyes, waiting, aching for his touch. Gentle, his fingers cupping, shaping the softness, his lips taking the swelling, rigid peak.

'I just want to touch you,' he groaned against her skin. 'Just for a moment, Maggie.'

She wanted it, too; wanted his hands on her, his lips inflaming her. His tongue moved softly over her nipples, sending her pulses pounding, her head swimming, her body twisting against his.

He found the button at the waist of her slacks, then she could feel his fingers against the roundness of her abdomen, trembling waves of sensation surging through her. In the next room, a spring creaked loudly and Michael's hand froze against her waist.

'Dixie,' she whispered.

His hand drew slowly away from her, then she was alone, lying on the sofa, her blouse open and pushed back. She was half naked, needing him still. She sat up, watching his back as he walked into the kitchen. What was he doing, for heaven's sake? Making coffee? It was *her* daughter on the other side of that closed door, but it was Michael who had pulled back first. How could he walk away?

What had he said to Dixie while they walked?

She pulled herself together, got her buttons done up and walked over to the big mirror on the sideboard. She combed her hair, trying not to let herself think of Michael in the next room.

In the mirror she could see him walking towards her. She couldn't read the expression on his face, couldn't tell what he saw in her reflected face. He stopped behind her, took her shoulders in his hands.

'I put coffee on,' he said, watching her, seeming to sense something sober. 'I think we could both use a cup.'

Maybe her eyes told him too many things, but she was afraid to talk. She didn't know what her voice would sound like. For an instant she thought she saw a flash of uncertainty or nervousness in his eyes. Then it was gone, and he squeezed her shoulders gently before he dropped his hands.

'Come and sit down, Maggie. No, I'm not going to make love to you again. Not tonight. I've shaken myself up enough for one night.' His eyes flared and she knew that he was seeing her naked in front of him, and that he wanted her badly.

'There's something I want to show you,' he said, taking her hand in his. She couldn't seem to pull away.

'Michael,' she whispered uneasily, 'you keep talking about marriage.' He walked away, picked up a large envelope he had set down when he first came in. He did not seem to hear her as she said tonelessly, 'I can't marry you.'

He walked back to her with the envelope, set it down on the coffee-table and sat beside her. She smoothed her hands on her thighs nervously. 'It's important for me to be able to look after Dixie and myself. Alone.' He took her hands in his own. She wished he hadn't, because it made it so much harder for her to think clearly.

'Don't confuse me with Dick, Maggie.' His thumbs caressed the backs of her fingers. She shook her head, but the silence was filled with his waiting, and his thumbs moving on her hands were like a spell woven by a hypnotist. She jerked her hands away, almost running as she stood up and went out to tend to the coffee he had started. He followed, leaning against the counter, watching with a frown on his face.

Michael covered her fingers with his, saying softly, 'I asked Dad about Dick the last time I was here. He told me—not everything, because of course he doesn't know everything. But enough.'

She followed him when he picked up the coffee mugs and carried them back to the sofa. 'Angus had no right to tell you. What I've told him, that was confidential. He should have——'

'He cares about you, Maggie. He wants you to be happy.'

Maggie shook her head. Michael's eyes were very gentle, and somehow she needed to hurt him. She said tightly, 'He still wants me back. He writes me, and he asks me to marry him again. He says——' She swallowed, too many memories getting out of hand. 'He always says that he loves me, that he needs me, and for a long time I was fool enough to think it was true, that——' She shrugged and said tightly, 'There's nothing worth talking about. Except to say that I can't do it again. I never want to be in that position again, married and dependent and helpless.'

Outside, a mournful horn sounded from a freighter in the harbour. Michael sat down beside her and she moved back, panicking. 'You've got to realise that I can't be dependent on anyone. Not ever again.'

'I love you, Maggie.' She shook her head in denial, but his low voice went on, 'No, darling. Don't say anything.

Not right now. Just see what I brought you.' He picked up the envelope and opened the flap, slipping out a thick sheaf of papers. He handed her a picture from the top.

'What is it?' She looked and saw boats berthed at a small marina. She took the next picture from his hands, found herself looking at a two-storey house that had seen a lot of love and life. Her hands were trembling and she dropped the picture on to the table. 'I don't get it, Michael. What is this?'

He held out another picture. 'It's a marina between Victoria and Duncan. Very pretty country. You can see it's beautiful. I've got the financial statements here for the last five years. It's not a bad little business. It's for sale.' He spread out some papers, said, 'I think it could do better than it has with a few new ideas and good management, but even as it is, it's a reasonable living.' She was staring at him, not asking or saying anything, watching his lips form the words. 'I put a deposit on it.'

'Why?' She pushed a shaking hand through her hair. The headache was back, but this time it was definitely emotional.

'Come on, Maggie! Why do you think?' He touched the worry crease on her forehead, smiling gently. 'Isn't that where you want to live? On the water? You want a job, financial independence.' He spread his hands and said, 'OK, darling, but not here! Not five hundred miles away from me.' He grasped her wrists gently and drew her hands away from her face. 'I've heard of commuting marriages, but Victoria to Prince Rupert is ridiculous! The jet service just isn't good enough. You can come south, work at your own marina.'

The pictures were all over the coffee-table, the marina he was buying for her. She stared at them dully. 'Didn't you think of asking me first?'

'I'm asking you now, Maggie.'

She shook her head, felt a welcome anger replacing something that felt like pain. 'No. No, you're not! You're telling me. Maggie wants a job, so you go out and buy one.' She pulled hands away, her voice trembling. 'I don't need someone to buy me a job! I can look after myself!' She got away from him, paced angrily across the room, swung back and found herself staring at him, her breath ragged. He was very still, watching her, no expression at all in those grey eyes.

'What am I supposed to say now, Mickey?' Her voice cracked with brittleness, her eyes flashed with something cold and furious. He didn't move or speak. 'I'm not going to let you buy me.'

He bent forward to straighten the papers on the coffee-table. His voice was muffled. 'Maggie, I love you and I'm trying to work out a way for us to be together.'

'No!' She caught a glimpse of herself in the big mirror. Surely she didn't look so nervously vulnerable as that? She swallowed, turned away to stare out of the sliding door to her patio. 'You want me,' she said flatly, talking to the walls. 'You're playing strategy games to get what you want, just as if I were Pederson Motors.'

She didn't give him more than a second to respond before she added forcefully, 'Did you think I would smile and say thank you for the nice present? I guess it really wasn't much of a risk. If I said no, you could hire someone to manage it, and you've got a paying asset to add to the growing MacAvoy empire.'

She was still shouting when she heard the door close. She turned back to the room, half expecting to find him there despite the evidence of her ears, but she was alone. She moved slowly to the sofa, anger draining away and leaving her limp and numb. She sank down. She could feel the warmth from Michael's body still clinging to the upholstery under her.

The envelope with its papers and pictures was gone, so he had taken the time to collect his things. He had left very quietly, only the sound of the door closing. If it were her, she would have slammed the door, but Michael had closed it quietly.

She had not realised that when he walked out of her door it would leave her so alone and trembling. It was long moments before she went to the door herself and opened it. There was no sign of Michael outside. The soft rain was falling on her face, mingling with her tears.

One light shone through a porthole in Angus's boat. She stepped on board, felt *Sasha* shift as she added her weight to the starboard side. The boat felt empty, silent except for the faint sound of Angus breathing quietly in his sleep. The light came from a kerosene lantern turned low. The wake from a boat passing shifted *Sasha's* floor underfoot as Maggie stepped down on to the cabin sole. The light swung gently on its gimbal, sweeping its glow across the cabin, illuminating the small piece of paper lying in the middle of the counter. She knew what the paper was as soon as she saw it. A note from Michael to his father:

'Dad, I've gone back to Victoria—driving back tonight in the rental car. Call if you need anything.'

There was no signature, and he did not mention her name at all. It was unlike him to give up and go away, so he must have decided she was not worth the effort. He would not be back—at least, not to see Maggie—and that was a relief.

Her ears were still ringing with the sound of her own voice shouting at Michael only moments ago, and it would be easy to decide that she was being unreasonable, pushing away a man who could make her feel so good just by talking to her over a telephone line. But she could not afford to make another rash marriage. She shivered, old ghosts welling up to smother her.

Memories swept over her . . . the lonely helplessness of being once more thrown on her own by Dick's unexpected abandonment. This time he had been fired from the grocery store job, and that meant she had to get out of their apartment.

She was both terrified and angry. He was never there when she needed him, and with Dixie's tears in her ears she vowed she would never need him again.

She packed her things and Dixie's, leaving anything that belonged to Dick behind. She had nothing, but she found shelter for herself and Dixie at a transition house for women. She knew that she had to do this on her own, that she must not turn helplessly to her parents. She was too old to become a child again.

One of the workers at the transition house found her a live-in housekeeping job with a family who were willing for her to bring Dixie into their home. It was not ideal, but she and Dixie could eat. When Dick turned up again, she refused to go back to him. She went to a lawyer and had a formal separation agreement drawn up, and somehow she found the strength to refuse Dick access to Dixie until he agreed to sign the agreement.

She applied for every job vacancy that she was even remotely qualified for. Eventually, she got a job working for the Fisheries and Oceans, and slowly she worked her way into a secure position. Today she was still paying Dick's bills from the days of their marriage, but that was the only hold he had on her.

There was no one in her life who had the power to leave her terrified and helpless just by walking out of the door, and that was the way she wanted it.

She left *Sasha* quietly. Angus never even knew she had been there. She went back to her house, closed the door behind herself and felt the loneliness washing over her.

Dixie was standing in the middle of the living-room, glaring at Maggie with an inexplicably hot fury, her hands on her hips as if she were about to deliver a lecture.

'Is he gone?' she demanded tightly. 'Is Mickey gone?'

She looks like me, thought Maggie. There's hardly anything of Dick in her. She said wearily, 'I suppose you heard us arguing.'

Dixie said defensively, 'You were shouting. It was you.'

Michael was always so controlled, and she was so damned emotional. He had probably realised that he was well rid of her by now.

'He wants to marry you,' accused Dixie. In a minute she was going to stamp her foot. Maggie walked back to that sofa, but she couldn't sit there, remembering Michael holding her, Michael kissing her, Michael handing her the pictures. She picked up the coffee-cup. It was almost full. She drank the cold liquid in one long, slow swallow.

'I need a father,' said Dixie abruptly. 'My daddy—you're not going to marry him again?'

Maggie winced. 'There's no question of that, Dixie. Your father and I are never going to be back together again. I've told you that.'

'But Daddy said——' She broke off, her face flushing.

Maggie's heart slammed against her ribcage. When had Dick seen his daughter? How? Behind her back? 'You've talked to your father? When? Last week? The afternoon you missed school?'

Dixie nodded and bit her lip. 'He came to the school at lunch. He said he wanted us back, that if I came with him, if——' She gulped and Maggie wanted to touch her, to comfort her. 'He said I should go home and pack my things an'—an' say I had a new friend and I was going to her for supper an'——'

Maggie set the cup down before it fell from her trembling hands. She hadn't even known. What had Dick been plotting? How dared he use Dixie like that?

'What happened?' she whispered.

'He said we'd all be together again, that we'd be a family and move into our own house on the hill and—I came home and you were busy and—I said what he told me, but you wouldn't let me go.'

There had been a fight over the fictitious Holly. A flaming row, and then Dixie had flung herself through the door and run off.

'I went there to meet him, but he was funny. Different from at school. He said we'd go away, and then we'd phone you, and you would come.' Maggie knew that Dick would have spent the afternoon drinking, waiting for Dixie to join him. Dixie went on, 'I told him we don't have a phone. He couldn't call you an' you'd be worried an' he——' The shadows crossed Dixie's face and Maggie knew how it had been. Dick laying on the emotional pressure, trying to make Dixie feel guilty. The girl looked so strong, so independent, but Maggie knew how hard it must have been for her to be strong enough to do what she felt was right and come back home.

Dixie was stiff when Maggie put arms around her, then she collapsed, sobbing, 'I'll never see him again. He's never going to forgive me, an' I'll never see him again. He was mad when I left, but there was no phone. That was before the phone got put in, and you'd be worried, an'—— He scared me, the way he was.'

Maggie trembled, thinking of all the things that might have happened. She took Dixie to the sofa, sat down in the same place where Michael been earlier. 'You did the right thing,' she said softly, careful of her words, knowing she had to divorce herself from her own feelings about Dick. 'Sometimes your daddy doesn't think straight, but he'll remember that he loves you. It might take a while, but one day there'll be a letter from him.'

She hoped it was true. She thought of the commercials on television. Childfind, they called it, advertisements searching for missing children. All those women, wondering where their children had gone. She could have been one of them. Dick knew they had no telephone. Had he really intended to call, or just to punish Maggie by taking Dixie away?

Dixie sniffled and gulped. 'He's not going to live with us again?'

'No, Dixie.' There should be words to soften it, but she couldn't think what.

'Mickey said I should tell you about it.' Dixie scrubbed tears away with her fist.

'Michael knew about this? You told him?'

'No, but he said I should talk to someone about what was botherin' me. You or him, or the counsellor at school. He said . . . He was nice, and I think you should marry him. So I can have a dad again.' She pushed the tears away, her eyes bright and defiant. 'I think he's nicer than Daddy, anyway, an' he likes me. He likes you, too.'

Maggie swallowed, knowing Dixie must not realise how much this affected her. 'Honey, I can't get married just to give you a father.'

Dixie squirmed in her arms and Maggie winced as a sharp elbow pressed into her side. 'Dixie, getting married is supposed to be for ever. Two people get married because——It isn't just for children. It has to be—it has to be because they're really in love.'

'Don't you love Mickey?' Dixie's eyes were clear and uncomfortably penetrating. 'You were kissing him. I saw you. You put your arms around him. You never let any of the other men kiss you like that. I watch out of the living-room window when Darryl brings you home.'

Maggie gasped, remembering how Michael had come so close to making love to her tonight, how his hands had pushed her clothes away, how his lips had taken possession of the softness of her breasts. Had Dixie seen that?

Dixie bounced impatiently on the sofa. 'So why don't you do what he wants? Why don't you get some boxes, an' we'll pack, an' then go to Victoria, an' you can have the marina, an'——'

'Dixie, you——' She couldn't tell Dixie that she was terrified of marriage. It would be unfair to load her own prejudices on to her daughter. She evaded, saying, 'You heard me shouting at him. You can't keep shouting at people, telling them to go away. Eventually, they—he went away.'

Dixie shook her head vigorously. 'You just got mad. It's just temper. He'll know you don't mean it.'

She shook her head. He must be furious with her to consider driving south on that long highway. It was not the kind of behaviour she would expect from Michael. It would be more like him to observe her anger, stop and think about it, then come back with a counterproposal.

Dixie was staring at her. Maggie said, 'Go to bed, honey. It's late, and we both need our sleep.'

'Are you——'

Maggie said firmly, 'Go to bed!'

When Dixie had closed the bedroom door behind herself, Maggie went to the stove and put more wood into it. It seemed very cold tonight. She put on a warm jacket and went outside on to the patio and stood, staring out over the water.

Michael would not come back. He was too good a businessman to keep playing in a losing game. She had refused his latest offer, and he would not put the price any higher to win her. He was gone, would only be back to tend to moving Angus home.

She was going to miss him terribly. She was afraid that she was going to spend her evenings watching that telephone. She should have it taken out, then she could not wait for his call. On Monday, she would go to the telephone office and arrange to have it disconnected.

CHAPTER TEN

MAGGIE was relieved when Dixie asked for permission to go to her friend's home for the day. She needed time alone, away from her daughter's silent disapproval. Time to think, too, because by sunrise this morning she had started to think of reasons for leaving Michael's telephone connected in her living-room. She had an uncomfortable feeling that it was past time for her to come to terms with her own feelings.

She walked slowly down the ramp to the floats, going carefully because it was steep and slippery today. She was trying to empty her mind of everything, trying to get rid of the panicky feeling of impending disaster that had been lurking ever since last night. Her mind was turning into a turmoil, a crazy mixture of worry about Dixie and Dick, and confusion whenever she thought of Michael.

'Hear the radio?' shouted the fisherman as he ran past. He looked both panicky and excited at the same time.

She knew with terrifying certainty that it was Michael. An accident, his car in the river! That highway had narrow, dangerous, twisting passages along the river. She felt such a terrible attack of loss that her arms clutched protectively around her stomach.

The fisherman shouted. 'Tsunami warning! Tidal wave!'

It wasn't Michael. Thank God!

She was grinning with relief and the fisherman was staring at her as if she had lost her mind. Perhaps she had, but she could handle a tidal wave more easily than

171

she could handle Michael injured—or dead.

As a light bursting over the horizon, she knew that anything would be easier to bear than the knowledge that Michael was gone for ever. Michael . . .

She was in love with him. If she lived another fifty years, she would still be in love with him.

She went to the wharfinger's trailer for her portable radio, acting automatically with her mind in a daze. Michael was gone, and she was the one who had sent him away. He had said that she would be a lonely old lady, or words to that effect. This morning, looking out over the boats that she had charge of, it seemed to her that she was well on the way to fulfilling his prediction.

She was just realising that last night she might have thrown away the most important thing in her life, but she had no time for realisations, no time for anything but the tsunami warning and its consequences. She called the coastguard on her portable radio, got the details on the tsunami warning as she went back down to Angus's boat.

They estimated three hours before the wave arrived at the mainland. No one had seen the wave, but the scientists were saying it could be ten feet high. What kind of damage would that do? Out at sea the water would simply rise ten feet, but near shore the wave could climb in one long, destructive sweep.

She wasn't sure what might happen to the wharfs, or to the boats. 'We don't know either, Maggie, said the radio operator. 'We don't even know if there is a wave. They've issued a warning, but there's nothing but empty ocean out there until the wave hits the Queen Charlottes, so no one knows for sure. We can't afford to ignore it. Try to get everyone to high ground, away from the waterfront. If they insist on being on their boats, get them out into the harbour, away from shore, in the deeper water.'

Thank God Dixie was already at Carol's, but she still had Angus to worry about, and he didn't want to leave the waterfront.

'I'll take *Sasha* out,' he insisted, oddly stubborn. 'The wave is coming at low tide. I don't expect it will amount to much.' Maybe he was right, but Maggie shuddered at the thought of Angus navigating the vessel in the dark. His eyes weren't good, and he had had trouble just taking *Sasha* over to the yacht club.

'I'll look after *Sasha*, Angus. I'll take her out into the harbour where it will be safe from the wave.' When he finally agreed, she called a taxi to take him up to Carol's, calling Carol's mother Joan to warn her that her home was turning into a tsunami refugee centre.

She came out of her house, standing still for mere seconds while she thought what to do first. There was so much to do. People would be coming down to take their boats out. She would have to check mooring lines for the unoccupied boats. This might be a disaster or it might be a false alarm. Either way, she had to do her job.

Then, later, she would have time to sit down and examine her own heart and mind. She and Michael had some very real differences that would have to be settled if they were to have a relationship. Marriage? Could she handle that? Could Michael compromise enough to let her retain her independence? Where was Michael now? Somewhere between Prince George and Vancouver? When would he get home?

On the next finger someone shouted, and she moved towards the voice to help in whatever way she could. The wind had started to come up, and there was a storm brewing, as if nature had picked up the growing tension.

What if she went to Michael, and he refused to talk to her? What could she say, quickly, before he shut the door in her face? He would remember how she had screamed at him, accusing him of trying to manipulate her. That was almost funny, because right now she was trying to figure out how to manipulate him, although God knew she wasn't very talented at it.

She managed to do a complete set of rounds in the next hour, checking that every boat left at the wharfs was well tied and had adequate fenders. When she was done, she went to the Sailing Association finger to help. The owner of one of the two biggest sail-boats was directing his wife and son in a complex, orchestrated sequence of manoeuvres. She had never realised it before, but the man looked a little like Michael. She had a crazy urge to touch him, or to cry.

'Get that line first!' the captain was shouting to his son. 'No! His aft line. We've got to open up at his bow, then hold him in while we get our boat out!'

No one knew for sure what would happen when the wave came, but everyone was coming, moving their boats out. There had been tidal waves in British Columbia in the past. One had done massive damage to Port Alberni, tearing wharfs from their dolphins, dashing boats up on shore.

The wind was rising and the captain of the big sail-boat was having a difficult time getting away from the wharf. Maggie was afraid he would collide with the smaller boat in front. She spent a frantic moment pushing the big brown hull away while the captain's wife pushed desperately from her deck. At last, the big monster slipped past, its stern just brushing the rail of the smaller boat as the helmsman gained enough speed to navigate away from the floats.

The wind was from the west now, the waves riding straight in behind the breakwater. Maggie kept her head down, stepping carefully on to the float. If she slipped and broke an ankle, she would be tied up with doctors and hospitals when every moment she was more certain that she should be trying to get to Michael. She grimaced, wondering if it might not be better to turn up on his doorstep in a cast. Would anyone slam the door on a woman with her leg in plaster?

When would she be able to go to him? Did he still want her? If so, then surely he was enough of a business-man to believe in making compromises to get what he wanted. What kind of compromise? Could she find a job in Victoria in time? Go to him there?

The docks were almost empty now. On her radio, the coastguard was announcing that the police would be coming down to clear people out of the waterfront area.

Michael might be home by now. Did she have time to telephone him before she took Angus's boat out of harm's way? She started towards the ramp, moving fast but placing her feet carefully on the slippery surface. When it rained, these boards could be like an ice rink.

She had her head down, watching where her feet went. She was not sure what made her look up. He was there on the main pier, standing still and watching her. She stopped dead, knowing that it must be a mirage, light waves bending and sending her his image from Victoria—or wherever he was.

He just stood there, not smiling, then she was run-ning, sliding on the float and not knowing or caring. She saw his arms open for her, and she lost control of her feet, careening, crashing into him. She heard him grunt as she collided against his chest, then she thought he laughed as his arms went around her and he bent to take her lips in a hard, hungry kiss that burned as his un-shaven face moved against her cold, wet skin.

'I love you,' she said as his lips left hers. The wind took her words away. As she said the words, she realised

how right they were. She and Michael—somehow they
would work it out. She shivered and pushed the fear
away. She was not a girl any more, not helpless and
dependent. She was a woman, and she was determined
to be strong enough to give herself to this man.

'I hoped you did.' His arms tightened on her. 'That's
what brought me back. Then, driving back, I heard the
radio. I was terrified I wouldn't get here in time.' He
didn't seem to realise that he was holding an armful of
cold, wet oilskins. She rubbed her cheek against his
bristly face, unable to take the tsunami seriously with his
arms around her. She rested her forehead against his
shoulder. Someone walked past. She didn't see who it
was, or even bother to look.

'Where's Dixie?' he asked.

'At Joan's—safe. Up on Hospital Hill.'

'Good.' He held her tightly. His face looked pale. He
had to shout to be heard over the wind. 'And Dad?'

'At Joan's, too.' His arms felt so good around her. She
wanted to lean her head against his shoulder, close her
eyes and forget everything else.

'All right. Let's get out of here.' He turned her
towards the ramp, but she pulled back.

'Michael, I can't. I have to take Angus's boat out in
the harbour.'

'What?' He looked astounded. 'You can't go out there!
They've issued a tsunami warning!'

She shook her head, feeling the cold rain all around.
His lips were growing thin and angry, and she was terrified that this would be the last straw. She pleaded, 'I
have to, Michael. I promised Angus I'd look after his
boat. It'll be safe out in the deep water, but it could get
dashed to bits here! When the tsunami hits——'

'Damn it, Maggie, you're the one I don't want dashed
to bits! There's a bloody tidal wave out there!' They

were glaring at each other, standing feet apart. Maggie saw his grey eyes hard and hot. She had never heard him so furious as when he shouted, 'God damn it, Maggie! It's just a bloody boat!'

She screamed, 'Don't shout at me!'

He was breathing quickly. 'I'd better not,' he agreed tightly. 'Because if we both lose our tempers we've had it. And you're going to lose yours for sure, aren't you?'

She licked her lips, tasting salt water mixed with the rain. She had missed him so terribly, yet here she was screaming at him, raging like a wild woman. And it was hopeless, because she would never change. 'I'm sorry, Michael. I'm sorry. I——'

'I'm getting used to it, darling.' He took her hand. His anger seemed to have seeped away. He asked patiently, as if to a child, 'Why is it that we have to take that boat out?'

She took a deep breath. 'He really can't manage the boat any more, Michael, but he loves it. I promised him I'd look after it.' She blinked, afraid that the tears would come freely now. She didn't want to cry in front of him.

Two RCMP officers came striding down the docks in unison, their boots thudding on the planks. 'Better clear out of here,' said one as he came up to Maggie and Michael. 'Oh, it's you, Maggie!' He frowned at her, said, 'There's not a damned thing you can do about your barge, Maggie. You'd need a tug to get it out of here, and there's no time.'

'I know,' she said. She had already thought of that, and knew that she had neither the time nor the money to hire a tug to move the barge to safety.

'We're taking a boat out on to the harbour,' said Michael slipping Maggie's arm through his. Then, as he led her towards Angus's boat, he asked, 'Are you friends with the whole damned police force up here?'

She didn't know why he was leading her towards Angus's boat instead of away from it, but it was only a minute later that he was holding her hand as she stepped aboard, saying, 'Careful! Don't fall, for God's sake!'

He moved to the cockpit and started the engine. *Sasha* started easily, as if she had been waiting for them. Even the wind gave no problem, pushing them away from the dock as Maggie let the lines go and Michael swung the tiller to steer around the barge that contained her home.

Michael was watching the lights ahead of them, muttering, 'Red's port, and green's starboard. Maggie, it's been years since I did much of this. We're in more danger from the teeming mess of boats out here than from any tidal wave.' He looked wonderful to her, standing at the tiller, peering out through the rain with his hair curling wetly and raindrops running down his cheeks and his neck.

'Michael, why are you doing this? A few minutes ago you were telling me I was crazy to be talking about taking this boat out.'

He held his dripping arm towards her and took her hand, bringing her close, his voice husky. 'He's my father, and you're right. I guess *Sasha* means a lot to him.' He looked away from the lights, down at her shadowed face. He added softly, 'If you would hold the tiller, I could kiss you properly.'

She brushed his cheek with her trembling lips. 'If you do, I couldn't possibly hang on to the tiller. Everything goes spinning when you kiss me.'

He grinned and took her lips, quick and hard. 'We've got a problem then, lady. Because any minute I'm likely to start making love to you.'

For a dizzying, beautiful moment there was only two of them in the universe. Then *Sasha* came up to the

wind with a sudden, wild lurch and Michael caught the
tiller and righted them, somehow managing to keep his
arm around Maggie as he did it.

'See what you're doing to me? I'm turning into a wild,
impulsive man. You're infecting me, Maggie. I wish
you'd known my mother. She was a lot like you.
Emotional, loving.'

Maggie asked wryly, 'Did she have a temper like I
have?'

'Not quite,' he admitted, 'but she had a weakness for a
gamble.' She knew this from Angus, but she had wanted
to hear it from Michael. He said, 'Not like some people,
who gamble away their homes, but she could never
resist buying a lottery ticket if she had a spare dollar and
someone was selling. Just after I went to university she
won the Irish sweepstakes. She bought *Sasha* for Dad.'
He was silent for a moment, remembering, then he said,
'It was a very special gift. They spent a lot of time
together here. I guess that's why he wanted to live here
after she died.'

She heard the emotion in his voice, and she wondered
how she could ever have thought that he would hurt
Angus. He had come to help, and he had been right.
Angus needed him now.

When Michael found a place where the water was
deep and they were a good distance from any other
vessel, he turned the engine off and let them float gently
and quietly. The rain had stopped and the wind had
dropped to a gentle coolness on their faces.

The water was so still, it was hard to believe in a
destructive wave. There was a long silence on the radio.
Maggie rested against Michael, content to let the time
move on without her. Later they would have to talk. She
would try to keep herself calm when that time came, but
she knew that her nervousness might catch at her

control and make her say things she would wish unsaid later. She could feel her uncertainties lurking in the background of her mind. Marriage. Hurt. The two seemed synonymous to her at times, but Michael was a very different man from Dick. Michael came when there was need, where Dick had always run away.

The silence grew and spread across the harbour. Everything was still. It was as if everyone was waiting, holding their breath. Then the peace was broken by the crackle of Angus's VHF radio.

'Security, security, security. All stations, all stations, all stations. This is Prince Rupert Coastguard Radio.'

The operator went on to announce in impersonal tones that the wave-height buoy on the Queen Charlotte islands had reported an insignificant half-meter fluctuation as the wave passed. The tsunami, the destructive tidal wave, had dwindled to a ripple. All around *Sasha*, engines revved up, lights started moving on the water. Maggie huddled close against Michael, wishing away the moment when they had to start moving with the others, going back to the wharfs and the people. She hoped he would kiss her first, before they started back to Angus's mooring.

The cockpit was faintly illuminated as a large fishing-boat steamed past them. Michael said carefully, 'Maggie, I don't want to go back. I want to be alone with you.'

She wanted that, too, but it was impossible. 'Dixie and Angus will be wondering what's happened.' His arm tensed around her and she was afraid he would move away from her. 'We could get the coastguard to telephone a message,' she suggested hesitantly.

Darkness surrounded them again. *Sasha's* navigation lights were just pinpoints in the night, not enough to penetrate the shadows where they sat together. 'Maggie,

I don't want either you or me to be able to walk out if we decide to get into another argument.'

She wished it were warmer, then she could take off the heavy rain slicker, curl close against him and feel his warmth. She touched his face and asked softly, 'Do you think we're going to argue?'

'Probably.' His voice hardened and he said, 'Last night I wanted nothing more than to get away from here. I'd done everything I could think of to persuade you—I kept telling myself that life would be a hell of a lot simpler without you, that I had had a lucky escape when you said no. Do you realise that you were in the middle of a dockside fight the first time I saw you? I think that's when you started turning my life upside-down, right then in the midst of the fight between Solly and Rex.'

She said weakly, 'Michael, I'm not always fighting.'

He seemed not to hear. 'I love you, but last night I was ready to give up.' His arm tightened. She could feel the tension in him, the desire, but he didn't lower his lips to hers. 'Then, somewhere in the middle of nowhere, I stopped driving. I stopped and stared at the trees for a long time. I guess I was thinking, but it seemed I was in a daze.'

She didn't know what to say, but she touched his face, her wet fingers feeling the roughness from his whiskers. His voice was suddenly harsh. 'Maggie, I can't remember wanting to cry since I was a child, but sitting there in the car last night, I . . . There was no point going back to Victoria. You weren't there. I had no choice but to come back here. I thought it would take for ever for me to get back. I tried to tell myself I should slow down, find a motel and get some sleep, but I had to get back to you. Then I heard the announcement on the radio that there had been another Alaskan earthquake and they were predicting a tsunami to hit the coast. And you were here.'

Michael was looking away from her, tension holding his shoulders rigid, and she knew there was nothing that mattered more than the man she loved. She touched his arm.

'Michael, there's a mooring buoy on the other side of the harbour, near Salt Lakes. We could tie to it.'

Michael started the engine, then Maggie called the coastguard and arranged for a message to be passed to Angus and Dixie by telephone. It was a moonless night, but when they neared the big buoy, they could see it looming up between them and the sky. Maggie found Angus's spotlight, and together they used a boat hook to catch the line on the buoy. Then they were floating, streaming away from the buoy in the current, securely fastened. Michael shut off the engine and the silence engulfed them totally. He followed her down below, lighting an oil lantern in the salon while she shed her wet rain gear.

'You, too,' she demanded, watching him move around the cabin, checking the level on the oil stove, turning the lantern down as it warmed and flared brighter. 'You're soaking, Mickey! Angus must have dry clothes that you could change into!'

She found a sweater and trousers in Angus's hatches, brought them back into the salon as Michael was stripping his wet shirt off. He dropped it on to the settee. The lantern sent golden light playing along the contours of his broad chest. His hands dropped to his belt. She could see the wet fabric of his trousers clinging to the heavy muscles of his thighs. She hugged Angus's clothes to herself, watching him.

'I hope you like what you see, Maggie.' His voice was low, almost a growl. He stepped closer, close enough to touch her. 'You're going to see a lot of me over the years.' His eyes were the cool grey she knew, but with a flame burning deep inside. She hoped he would always look at her like this, as if she were the most beautiful woman in the world.

'Michael . . .' She managed to hold the clothes out to him. He took them, put them aside on the table. 'Michael, I'm terrified.'

He shook his head. 'Love me, Maggie, and fight me if you have to, but don't run away from me. Don't ever run away from me or hide from me again.'

She thought she would drown in his eyes. He saw right through her. He always had. He was waiting, standing very still.

Maggie said, 'Once this was over—this tsunami thing—I think I was going to you as soon as I could. To your house, or your office, or wherever you were.' He didn't touch her. She wished he would take her in his arms again. When he touched her, she knew she could say nothing wrong, do nothing wrong.

The muscles of his chest tensed to rigidity under the yellow glow of the lantern. What did he want her to say? She said hurriedly, 'I wasn't going to—I didn't want there to be anyone in my life with the power to hurt me. It seemed safer that way. If I didn't fall in love, I couldn't get hurt too badly. I—I never realised I could feel like this, the way I love you. I thought—I had no idea how it would hurt when you went away.'

He seemed to be having trouble with his breathing. She wondered if his heart was thundering the way hers was. His voice was ragged as he said, 'Maggie, after I went home from that first weekend—when I kissed you and you bit my lip—I tried to tell myself that I'd been hit by some temporary madness. My life was very stable, very much in my control. I didn't love Sam, and I really didn't think she loved me, but it was comfortable and convenient. But I couldn't seem to forget how you had felt in my arms, how your eyes glowed green when you were angry or aroused. Despite your anger, Maggie, I knew you had felt what I'd felt when you were in my arms.'

'Yes,' she admitted shakily, 'but I was furious that you thought you could just grab me, take what you wanted from me.'

He pushed his drying hair back with a trembling hand. 'I knew as soon as I saw you again that I had to do something. I couldn't seem to think of anything except my need to get close to you. I—Maggie, I'm not very proud of it, but I had the idea that if I could make love to you, just once, I could be free of this madness you'd put on me.'

She had taken her wet shoes and socks off. She was standing in bare feet, making him seem much taller than he had before. 'I thought the same thing,' she whispered, her eyes glowing green in the flickering lamplight. 'When you took me home after we went dancing, I was going to let you make love to me. I thought I'd be able to forget you then.'

He was looking through her, remembering. 'When we went inside your house and found Sam there, I thought I would die of the frustration of needing you. I knew there was no way I could continue a relationship with Sam, feeling the way I did. My world was crazy, Maggie. I'd met you and suddenly I seemed to be behaving like a heel to everyone around, and I hardly knew what was going on. I took Sam to a café and told her it was over. I made a mess of that, but all I could think of was getting back to you.'

She remembered how she had trembled, listening to him calling her through the door, how she had opened it only to send him away. 'Michael, I couldn't let you back in that night. I was terrified you would see how you were affecting me, and I felt terribly shaken that I'd wanted another woman's man so desperately. I was confused, and I guess I was terrified because I had started falling in love with you—although I didn't admit that to myself until today.'

He took her face in his hands, massaging her temples with his thumbs. 'Everything is shadows without you, Maggie. Making love with you was incredibly wonderful, but it wasn't enough. That night, at the hotel, I realised that I wanted to share everything with you, to find you in my bed in the mornings, to help you get Dixie through her teens. It seemed to me that the only answer was for you to come home with me, to marry me. I was so sure it was right, I couldn't believe it when you refused and then ran off with that policeman. Damn, Maggie! I could have killed you that night!'

'I won't run again,' she promised, her jaw moving against his hands as she spoke. 'I'll stay and we'll work it out.'

'Or fight it out,' he agreed in a low, sensuous voice that made her shiver with anticipation. 'Maggie, you accused me of treating you like a corporate takeover. That made me furious, but you were right. When I asked you to marry me, to live with me, and you said no, I went home and sat down to plan it, just like the Pederson deal. The marina was my next move. It—I hadn't thought that I was trying to buy you. I just wanted you, and I was trying to fit you into my life.' He grinned. 'I guess I just assumed that if anyone's life had to change, it should be yours, and I didn't see why you shouldn't go along with that if I made it attractive enough, gave you enough.'

'You scared me,' she admitted on a whisper, touching

his chest with one tentative hand. 'I can't help it, but when I think about walking away from my job, the fear wells up and I sometimes feel like I'm back to the days when I wasn't sure if I could make it, if I could look after Dixie, support us, or——'

He took her hand, trapped it against the matted, damp hair on his chest. 'Maggie, I want to be with you. I don't want to threaten you. I don't want to take away anything you need.' He let her hand go, used both arms to draw her very gently against him. 'Last night, staring at a bunch of trees in the middle of nowhere, I realised that there's nothing in my life that matters more than you. Just love me, Maggie,' he whispered, pressing his lips against her eyelids to close her eyes. 'Just let me love you. We'll work it out.'

The boat rocked softly under their feet. Michael shifted, balancing himself against the galley counter, welcoming the feel of Maggie's weight against him. She said, 'I'll come to you. Dixie and I can come. I can give my notice.'

She could feel the uneasiness threatening her, but she was determined to overcome reactions that belonged to Dick and to the past. 'I keep feeling frightened of being back in that helpless situation, abandoned and broke. I've just got to keep fighting that.' He found her lips with his, making it impossible for her to talk for a moment. She was breathless, almost incoherent, saying, 'Michael, are you sure you know what you're getting into? I might not be very good at being your wife. My bank account's always overdrawn. And your sister terrifies me, and if I have her to dinner, I might spill the peas in her lap.'

He pushed her damp pullover up, moved her arms like a child's as he stripped the heavy, wool garment away from her. 'I hope you do,' he said as he fumbled with the buttons of the blouse he found underneath. 'She terrifies me, too. Sometimes, I think there's a human being under all that hair spray and make-up, but I'm never quite sure.' When he pushed the blouse away from her shoulders, she was standing in his arms in only her bra and slacks. He dropped his arms away and looked at her, as if looking were enough.

Trembling, she said huskily, 'I hope you like what you see.'

'The first time I touched you . . . You were standing there on the docks, and you kissed Darryl.' His voice was so low, she had to strain to hear it. 'I hardly knew you, and I couldn't believe what I felt when you went into his arms. I wanted to tear him away from you.' He tried to laugh at himself, but his lips wouldn't curve and his eyes were burning. 'I'm not used to losing control of my feelings, Maggie. I've never had feelings like this before.' He touched her very gently, almost hesitantly. He whispered. 'I think I'm going to love you for ever.'

She flowed up against him and reached her arms up to pull his head close. She moved her lips softly against his. When his mouth hardened and took control of hers, she softened against him. He was trembling when he put her aside.

'First,' he said hoarsely, 'I'm going to shave. Then, I'm going to make love to you. Very slowly. Until you're crying out my name when I touch you. Until I look into your eyes and see nothing there except me—you needing me.'

He left her trembling and went into the head to shave. She could still feel the words he'd spoken, like a promise, flowing through her veins like fire.

She found a towel in the galley and dried her hair. She took off her wet jeans. She wished she could find a sexy, filmy nightgown to put on, but instead she found a big, oversized shirt in Angus's hanging locker. She combed her hair, and she put the shirt on over her panties and bra. She left the top two buttons open, hoping that he would see the curve of her breasts through the open neckline and want her even more when he saw her. She wished she had a seductive perfume to put on.

The door opened. He was wearing Angus's dry jeans. He hadn't put the shirt on. She stood, trembling, waiting, for him to come to her.

'You look very beautiful,' he said. She couldn't say a word. He came to her, took her into his arms. 'Don't be afraid, sweetheart.' She wanted to tell him that she would follow him anywhere, that the fears were nothing beside the joy of having him beside her.

'We can work it out,' he promised. He brushed her hair back from her face with gentle fingers, his voice caressing her. 'Somewhere in our negotiations, Rory Pederson offered to buy me out. When he made the offer, I laughed, but last night I realised that it was a way for me to be with you. I can always take him up on it. Be a bit of a twist, wouldn't it? I try to buy him out, so he ends up buying me.'

She found her voice. 'That's crazy!'

'Not really. It would be fitting. Both my takeover bids turned around on me! He offered a good price. I could get something else going up here. We could buy a house—or a bigger barge, if you're stuck on living on the water. If so, we'd better get an oil furnace, and a bigger house on it, because I think Dad might be living with us. You won't mind that, will you?'

'No. Of course not. I—Michael, you can't do that! That's insane! The marina made more sense. I'd have to learn something about the business end of it, but the rest I know I could do. You know the business part. And——'

He shook his head. 'Maggie, I want you to be happy. I spent too long being selfish, not thinking of you. No, darling, we'll settle it tomorrow. Or the next day. Right now . . .' He found her shape through the soft flannel of the shirt. 'Right now, we've something far more important to do.' He slipped his hands under the loose shirt, his fingers spreading over the soft flesh that covered her waist and back.

She drew in a deep, ragged breath, saw his eyes locked on the movement of her breasts under the shirt. 'Tomorrow,' she agreed, letting her hands roam freely on his bare chest. Her head tipped back, her body needing his for support, her throat exposed for his lips.

'Love me, Mickey,' she whispered. He bent his lips to her, caressing her white throat, then he took her up in his arms and carried her through the narrow passageway to the master stateroom of *Sasha*.

While the sea flowed under them he made love to every part of her, hands and lips and body loving each sensitive, passionate part of his woman until she was crying out his name, trembling hot and wild in his arms, sending him beyond control, touching him with fire and love, joining them together . . . for ever.

Harlequin Presents

Coming Next Month

1183 HEAT OF THE MOMENT Lindsay Armstrong
Serena's first encounter with Sean Wentworth is embarrassing—so she's surprised to get the job of looking after his nephews at his remote Queensland station. Her relationship with Sean is just beginning to blossom when the past catches up with her.

1184 TRUE PARADISE Catherine George
If Roberto Monteiro chooses to think Charlotte used her female charms to gain her own—or her father's—ends, let him. Once he leaves the neighborhood she needn't see him again. Then Roberto insists that Charlotte come to Brazil with the contract....

1185 STORMY ATTRACTION Madeleine Ker
Paula prepares to do everything she can to keep the small island paradise off Majorca from development. She hadn't known her opponent would be charming Juan Torres—or that her heart would be at war with her convictions!

1186 THE THIRD KISS Joanna Mansell
Separated from her holiday group in Egypt, Bethan is rescued by Max Lansdelle. Only after she blackmails him into letting her stay in his camp does she realize that Max is not the cool customer she thought he was.

1187 PRISONER OF THE MIND Margaret Mayo
Lucy blames arrogant businessman Conan Templeton for her father's death and is horrified when she has to act as his secretary. So why is she disappointed when theirs seems likely to remain only a business relationship?

1188 A QUESTION OF LOVE Annabel Murray
Keir Trevelyan finally tracks down his dead brother's child, but Venna isn't going to give up her half sister's daughter that easily. She pretends to be a reckless mother with loose morals. Naturally, she's trapped by her own deception....

1189 WHITE MIDNIGHT Kathleen O'Brien
Amanda is desperate to be rid of Drake Daniels when he invades her family's Georgia estate, flaunting his new wealth. She once gave him everything—and paid the price.

1190 A DIFFERENT DREAM Frances Roding
Lucilla Bellaire wants success and is prepared to go to any lengths for it—or so she thinks. When Nicholas Barrington is neither bowled over by her beauty nor repelled by her ruthlessness, she faces a situation she can't cope with.

Available in July wherever paperback books are sold, or through Harlequin Reader Service:

In the U.S.
901 Fuhrmann Blvd.
P.O. Box 1397
Buffalo, N.Y. 14240-1397

In Canada
P.O. Box 603
Fort Erie, Ontario
L2A 5X3

Janet DAILEY

THE MASTER FIDDLER

Jacqui didn't want to go back to college, and she didn't
want to go home. Tombstone, Arizona, wasn't in her
plans, either, until she found herself stuck there en route
to L.A. after ramming her car into rancher Choya Barnett's
Jeep. Things got worse when she lost her wallet and
couldn't pay for the repairs. The mechanic wasn't
interested when she practically propositioned him to get
her car back—but Choya was. He took care of her bills and
then waited for the debt to be paid with the only thing
Jacqui had to offer—her virtue.

Watch for this bestselling Janet Dailey favorite, coming in
June from Harlequin.

Also watch for *Something Extra* in August and *Sweet
Promise* in October.

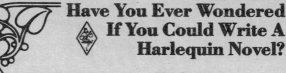

Have You Ever Wondered If You Could Write A Harlequin Novel?

Here's great news—Harlequin is offering a series of cassette tapes to help you do just that. Written by Harlequin editors, these tapes give practical advice on how to make your characters—and your story— come alive. There's a tape for each contemporary romance series Harlequin publishes.

Mail order only

All sales final

ANNOUNCING . . .

The Lost Moon Flower
by Bethany Campbell

Look for it this August
wherever Harlequins are sold

Harlequin Regency Romance™

Romance the way it was *always* meant to be!

The time is 1811, when a Regent Prince rules the empire. The place is London, the glittering capital where rakish dukes and dazzling debutantes scheme and flirt in a dangerously exciting game. Where marriage is the passport to wealth and power, yet every girl hopes secretly for love....

Welcome to Harlequin Regency Romance where reading is an adventure and romance is *not* just a thing of the past! Two delightful books a month.

Available wherever Harlequin Books are sold.

REG-1R